Want a behind-the-scenes journey of me as a writer?
The ups and downs, new deals, book sales, giveaways and more? I share it all! Join the exclusive Southern Sleuths private group today! Go to www.patreon.com/Tonyakappesbooks

As a special thank you for joining, you'll get an exclusive copy of my cross-over short story, *A CHARMING BLEND.* Go to Tonyakappes.com and click on subscribe at the top of the home page.

Wildlife, Warrants, & Weapons

Southern Hospitality with a Smidgen of Homicide

It creams my corn to think I've been accused of murder.

I'm a handyman in the Daniel Boone National Park. My main employer is Mae West, at the Happy Trails Campground.

When I got a phone call to take down some trees on this guy's property for a side hustle, I jumped at the chance. That's one of the biggest money-making jobs around these parts.

Unfortunately, I got hauled off to jail after I was accused of being part of an illegal logging crew. Simply enough, I gave Sheriff Hank Sharp the name of the man who hired me, but he was found murdered by one of my tools.

Not only am I accused of illegal logging, now I'm the number-one suspect in this man's murder.

It just creams my corn to be accused of murder.

There's only one person I trust to get me out of this mess, and that's Maybelline West.

I'm sure she, along with her nosy friends, the Laundry Club Ladies, will snoop around to help clear my name.

CHAPTER ONE

A calmness had fallen over Happy Trails Campground after a very busy spring season. The seasonal rain had finally come to an end, leaving a trail of vibrant colors that'd painted the Daniel Boone National Forest.

I'd been getting ready for the wedding of Bobby Ray Bond, my foster brother, and Abby Fawn, one of my best friends, over the last few months. Tomorrow was the big day. But today, I had to focus on the maid of honor, me, getting together with the bridesmaids.

I swore it was a made-up gig. When Abby told me one of my duties was to host the event, I had no idea what I was in store for, much less the cost associated with such an event.

Of course, after Mary Elizabeth had gotten word I was in charge of such a joyous occasion for her future foster daughter-in-law—mm-hmm, Mary Elizabeth was my and Bobby Ray's foster mother until she adopted me—she plunged her Southern hands all up in the event, and here I stood, in front of my camper van with a jug of Mary Elizabeth's sweet tea in each hand, about to make my way over to the large white tent she'd insisted we get for the festive occasion.

"Let's go." I looked down at Fifi, my toy poodle. "Don't you dare jump in the lake," I warned.

Fifi loved to jump into the lake and swim around with the ducks. I had no time between now and tomorrow, the wedding, to give her a bath.

Did y'all think she really listened to me? Heck no. As soon as I took a step to go up to the front of Happy Trails Campground, the campground I owned, she darted off and took a flying leap in the air before I could scream.

"No!"

Too late. She was happily paddling around with her head stuck out of the water, sights on the ducks, swimming their way.

"She never listens," I groaned and headed up the road to the front of the campground, where the white tent was set up in the grass between the recreational center building and the tiki bar.

A few times, I glanced over at the lake and couldn't help but smile at Fifi. She'd stolen my heart a few years ago after she wiggled herself into a situation that left her homeless. If truth be told, Fifi was my bestest friend, not the Laundry Club Ladies.

"I can't believe it's finally here." Abby was standing up near the long banquet table at the far end of the tent, smack-dab in the center of our group of friends.

The Laundry Club Ladies.

Our group consisted of Betts Hager, Dottie Swaggert, and Queenie French, along with honorary members Mary Elizabeth Moberly and Dawn Gentry.

"Here's our maid of honor now." Abby smiled so brightly. Her long brown hair was down and flowed over her shoulders, which was rare to see since she literally wore it up in a ponytail almost every day. "It's gorgeous."

She waited for me to put the jugs of tea on the table before she gave me a giant-size bear hug.

"You do know this was all of Mary Elizabeth's doing, right?" I didn't want to take credit and gave credit where it was due.

"I just put a little bit of Southern magic on it." Mary Elizabeth's fingertips grazed the strand of pearls around her neck before she clasped her hands in front of her, resting them perfectly against her pink short-sleeved Lily Pulitzer cardigan, which lay at the waistband of the white Lily Pulitzer pants with little yellow-and-green pineapples embroidered all over them.

Her eyes swept up and down me, giving me the judgy Southern-mama vibe that my wardrobe of choice didn't suit the occasion. I pinched a grin, and instead of poking the bear, which in this case was Mary Elizabeth, I kept my mouth shut.

"Tea?" I unscrewed the lid, filling the air with the sweet smell of sugary tea, knowing Mary Elizabeth had really outdone herself on this batch.

I filled the glass tea flutes halfway since that was the Southern-etiquette way to do things. I should know. Mary Elizabeth had spent a pretty penny on etiquette lessons for me, and though I rarely practiced them in my daily life, I knew when to put the lessons to good use.

When she was around.

"This looked like it cost a pretty penny." Smoke rolled out of Dottie's mouth.

"Yeah. I had no idea what an event of such fanciness would cost." I kept a static grin on my face so Mary Elizabeth wouldn't notice.

"I bet you wished you'd kept that little velvet bag of diamond we found in your old penthouse instead of just willy nilly handin' them over to the FBI." Dottie took a drawl off the cigarette and blew out a long steady stream.

"I might've kept one or two if I'd known how much being a maid of honor was going to cost me." I winked at her, teasing of course.

There was no way I was going to keep the bag of diamonds Dottie and I had found when we took a little visit to New York City. They weren't mine to keep and though it was pretty tempting, it would've been bad karma and I needed Paul West to be out of my life for good. He'd proven to be more of a pain in the you know what dead then he was living. With those diamonds in the hands of the authorities, I didn't have to worry about Paul or his illegal dealings anymore.

Boy oh boy, I thought to myself, *it would've been nice to have just one of those diamonds to pay for all of this.* I looked around.

Underneath the white tent was a long banquet table, a small gaslight fireplace, and a s'more stand for later tonight. We were all staying in the campground at one of the bungalows I'd reserved for this special night.

Henry Bryant, my handyman; Dottie; and I had strung thousands of twinkly lights around the top and poles of the tent. We'd gotten them from Buck down at the Tough Nickel Thrift Shop in downtown Normal, the small rural Kentucky town we lived in.

The lights were strung across the ceiling of the tent and dangled down like a little cobweb of romantic lights. If we weren't having the wedding at the Milkery, I would've suggested we have it all here since it truly had a magical and romantic feel.

The large barnwood table in the middle of the tent looked gorgeous with a white runner down the middle and was the perfect fit for fifteen long stemmed light-pink taper candles. The milk-glass vases glowed from the flickering candles. All the romantic vibes coursed through me at the sight of the pops of hot-pink, pale-pink, and white roses. It truly was a special event for Abby.

The setup wouldn't have gone off without Mary Elizabeth arranging, rearranging, and arranging again to give it the perfect Southern flair.

She'd told me that it wasn't every day your son gets married, so she pulled out all the stops even though Bobby Ray wasn't her birth child. She loved me and him like we were, and for that, I was grateful.

"Toast." Mary Elizabeth nudged me with her elbow before she lifted her glass in the air.

"Oh, yeah." I, too, followed suit and lifted my glass up in the air. Everyone else joined me. "Abby, when I first met you the day I rolled into town—a new RV'er, broke, with no friends and what I thought was no family—you embraced me in the first hug."

Long, happy sighs escaped everyone as I continued.

"I remember you telling me that we hugged around here. You've done more than hug me. You took me in when I didn't deserve a friend.

4

WILDLIFE, WARRANTS, & WEAPONS

You did all of this with your fantastic marketing skills when I didn't have a dime to pay you." I glided the glass in the air, gesturing to the campground. "You loved a family that I didn't know still loved me." I glanced over at Mary Elizabeth, who happened to find me after I'd disappeared from her life many years ago, but all of that was water under the bridge. "And your heart opened up to a man who believed in me and became the big brother I needed. That's what you've done for just me in the few years I've known you. I can't imagine what you've done for everyone here. But I can say without a doubt that I can speak on behalf of our group of family"—I did think of Betts, Abby, and Queenie as my family—"that we are thrilled for you. The happiness you wear is shown daily. The joy in your relationship is something that gives me hope that one day, I will be happy too. Your relationship has become an example to me and, I'm sure, everyone here." My voice cracked as I thought of my relationship with Hank Sharp, which had come to what felt like the end. "I'm so excited and honored to have a sister that I can walk through the rest of my life with, that I also consider a best friend."

I held the glass up a little longer in the air. There were a few sniffles, but I didn't look to see who was crying.

"To our beautiful, thoughtful, and amazing friend, Abby. May you continue to enjoy a lifetime of happiness. Cheers!"

There wasn't a dry eye amongst us, especially after everyone had gone through and given a little speech.

We all turned after we heard some gravel spitting up underneath some tires and gave little yelps of joy when the Pamper Camper mobile spa came around the corner and stopped in front of the tent.

"You didn't." Abby jerked around, dancing in place, squealing in delight after I gave a hard confirmation nod.

The spa idea was all mine, and I was happy to have done it for Abby.

The door of the mobile spa popped open.

"Where's our bride?" Glenda Russel stood in the camper van. Her long red hair flowed down the sides of her face with a strand of braids fixed around her head like a band. She was so lovely for an older woman. She had the most unusual features, with the combination of her hair color, gray eyes, and olive skin.

"I see her." Tex, Glenda's partner and local chiropractor, appeared behind Glenda.

She stepped out of the camper van, giving us a full view of Tex.

Shirtless. His usual attire. His shorts were so snug his muscles bulged along with the veins in his thighs. I was sure if Tex could get away with being a nudist, he would.

"I'm ready to do some reiki." Vigorously, he rubbed his hands together and pointed at Mary Elizabeth. "You're first."

He grabbed a folded-up reiki table and left the camper van. He headed over to the far side of the tent, where he quickly unfolded the table.

Mary Elizabeth blushed and giggled before she did a little giddy up toward the makeshift reiki station while Tex got all the sheets, oils, and special smelly good things he liked to use on his clients.

"Is our bride ready?" Glenda gestured for Abby to follow her into the mobile spa.

There was an inward peace settling in my gut right before I heard more gravel spitting up underneath some tires.

Since I was technically working the campground offices and Dottie was enjoying another glass of sweet tea while sucking down her cigarette, I looked over my shoulder to see if it was one of the campground guests and if I needed to go over to greet them.

It wasn't.

The sheriff's car pulled up and around the lake.

My heart sank when I saw it was Sheriff Hank Sharp. I wasn't really sure what I'd call him. But I knew it was no longer *boyfriend*.

CHAPTER TWO

"Still not good?" Betts Hager sidled up to me when she noticed what I had noticed.

"Not bad, but not back together." I shrugged and turned away when I saw he had driven past my camper van, not really sure where he was going since he'd recently gotten his camper fixed up and decided not to move back into Happy Trails Campground.

Happy Trails Campground was not a mobile home subdivision as some had thought it was when I first moved here to take over. It was a real campground for tourists to stay in the Daniel Boone National Park. When I found out I was the owner and moved here from New York City after a long history of how I'd gotten the campground, there were already people who'd set up their camper and called it home.

There were just a few, like Dottie Swaggert, Ty Randal, Bobby Ray, me, and Henry Bryant. We also had a few seasonal guests who liked to keep their campers here but paid me the lot fees each month. Mostly, the campers were tourists who would rent for a week or so.

The campground was fully equipped, meaning we offered water hookup, electric, internet, continental breakfast, several camping packages, outdoor activities, and an entertainment venue. We welcomed all sorts of guests.

They were able to drive in their own campers, tent camp, or rent a bungalow if they didn't like to camp.

Tonight, I had one of the bigger bungalows for us to stay in so we could all wake up refreshed before we headed off as a group to the Milkery for the wedding.

"What's Hank want with Henry?" Queenie pinched a piece off of a sugar cookie in the shape of a wedding bell into her mouth and threw a chin toward Henry Bryant's camper.

"Not sure. Maybe some handyman work?" I suggested and tried not to act as if I cared too much.

Even though I tried not to look, my eyes had a mind of their own. The empty campground lot where his camper had sat for the better part of two years was occupied by someone from Minnesota. Every time I looked at the spot, it was hard to not imagine his camper there. Last I'd heard, he'd gotten a little plot of land real cheap down on Soggy Bottom Road.

Just then, another car pulled up, and Rebecca Fraley from the National Parks Office got out.

She waved something in the air at me.

"Excuse me. She's dropping off the new summer-season flyers," I told the group and headed up to the front of the office, where she was waiting for me.

"What's going on down there?" She teetered back and forth around me to see Hank's car in front of Henry's camper.

"I'm not sure." I didn't want to get into it with her.

Rebecca was a tad bit nosy, and I'd learned that from having to deal with her at the National Parks Office when I was there for the committee meetings now that I was on the board.

"Are those the new brochures?"

"Hot off the press. I thought I'd swing by on my way home and drop them off since I'm sure you're packed for the rest of the summer." She handed them to me but kept one back. She unfolded it. "I think they turned out nice this year. Here's your ad and the coupon for the kayak lessons."

"Oh, it does look great." I was pleased as pie with it. "The colors are nice and bright."

"We ended up going with a new printing company this year, and I think everyone is going to love them. I have another stack at the office for when you run out."

"Thanks for dropping them off. I'm hosting Abby's night before wedding with the bridesmaids, so I better get back." I was happy Rebecca dropped these by. It saved me from having to go by there at the beginning of the week. "Thanks again."

"No problem. Tell Abby I'm sorry I can't make the wedding. We have a new ranger at the office who transferred from another district, and I've got to do his paperwork. I told them it could wait, but they insisted. I sure hate missing the fun." She shook her head.

"I'll save you a piece of cake. I promise. That's the good stuff anyways." I laughed and thanked her again.

I set the brochures inside the office and returned to the group. Hank was still at Henry's camper, talking to him.

"Something looks funny." Betts sighed and put her arm around me, using her hands to turn me away. "We aren't going to worry about boys today."

"Yeah, but I worry about Henry." There was a ping in my gut. I didn't know a whole lot about Henry or his family.

Henry was my employee, and he did great work. I never had to question him on anything or ask him to do anything. Dottie and I would collect little to-do lists during our daily walks around the campground. When we'd get back, we wrote those on one of the wipe-off boards in the office, and Henry would check them off as he did his usual necessary work.

Just by listening to him and Dottie talk, I knew he did side work for others on his time off. I wouldn't put it past Hank, now that he was busy being the sheriff of Normal, to need Henry to do some work around his new place. Hank was never one to get people to do work for him since he loved to do all the physical activity himself. He claimed it was how he kept in good shape, but I was only speculating that he needed Henry for some odd job.

It was a big deal after Hank and me, well, I'd decided Hank and I needed some time apart.

Not that I was ready for a family, which meant children, nor was I sure I wanted children, but Hank didn't. He'd not had the best father in the world, and he didn't see himself as being a father. I, on the other hand, wasn't sure what I wanted and didn't want to place that on Hank after it was all said and done—ring on the finger, living together, then *wham* I wanted to have a child, which would explode his world.

So it was me that told him I needed some time. But I wasn't sure what I needed or how long.

I was grateful for Abby and Bobby Ray's wedding to distract me. I'd put any sort of feelings I had on the back burner and would gladly keep them there for a few more days. It was easy to do that when he didn't live here and I didn't have to run into him.

"Don't give him the satisfaction of lookin' his way, May-bell-ine." Dottie had a way with words.

"Oh, Dottie. Mae needs to do what her heart is telling her," Betts cut in.

"Listen to me, Betts Hager." Dottie bent over at her waist slightly and wagged a finger at Betts. "You sweep your own back porch before sweeping somebody else's."

"What does that mean?" Betts pulled her shoulders back.

"You know what that means." Dottie's eyes snapped before she took her cigarette case out of her waistband and lit up a new smoke. Her eyes glaring at Betts were barely visible as the vapors curled out of her mouth.

"I forgive you." Betts jerked away and darted off toward the Pamper Camper.

"Seems to me like you're forgiving everybody who has wronged you." Dottie threw her words to Betts's back.

Betts stopped. Her hands were at her sides and balled into fists as though she were trying to gain her composure before she continued to walk and disappear into the mobile salon without looking back once.

"That was uncalled for. Why couldn't you just keep your mouth shut until after tomorrow?" Queenie French twirled her fanny pack around her waist to the front and unzipped it to get out her lip balm.

"Whut?" Dottie's hillbilly slang accent came out in full force when she was offended. "It seems to me that Betts has forgiven Lester after him killin' someone, not to mention cheatin' on her."

"Huh?" I was taken so off guard by Dottie's comment that I didn't notice what was going on with Hank and Henry at Henry's camper.

"Mm-hmm. Talk around town is Betts has been havin' them con-ju-gal visits." Dottie made a face like she'd been sucking on a dill pickle. "And by the reaction she just had, I'm guessin' what I've heard is true."

"Are you sure?" I questioned since Betts hadn't even told me that. "I know she'd started the Bible-thumpers prison group back up, and I'd gone to see Lester when I needed that information." I didn't have to recall the information to them since we'd all been snooping around after there was a murder in town.

"She's using that rinky-dink of a church bus to cover up her longin' for him." Dottie was making some serious accusations.

"It's not our tale to tell, Dottie Swaggert." Queenie turned back to me. "Honey, how are you doing these days?"

Queenie was good at changing the subject or at least trying to, but she didn't need to. Hank Sharp did that for us as we rubbernecked to get any sort of glance at Hank's car as it passed by us.

I kept my eyes on Hank, but he didn't appear to look my way. Or at least his face didn't turn to look out the window. He had on his sunglasses, so his eyes could've shifted my way.

Either way, I pulled up to stand a little taller.

"What on earth?" Queenie questioned. "Is that Henry Bryant in the back of Hank's car?"

I glanced in the back window as the car drove past and noticed a ball cap.

Henry Bryant's ball cap.

"My hair is standing up forty ways to Sunday." Mary Elizabeth had shuffled up behind us without us noticing.

She had her fingertips dug into her hair, trying to fluff it back up.

"What?" She looked between us before she leaned around us to see what we were all staring at. "Is that Hank Sharp? Did someone die? Seeing he only comes 'round here now when there's been a murder." She snickered.

"We aren't sure." I looked around the group and wondered just why on earth Hank Sharp would be hauling Henry Bryant out of the campground in the back of his sheriff's car.

"What?" Mary Elizabeth brought her hands to her heart. "Oh dear, not on Bobby Ray's wedding weekend." She lifted her hand and fanned her face as though she were about to pass out. "Who's going to make sure the grass is a perfect one-and-a-half inches at the Milkery if Henry is in jail?"

CHAPTER THREE

With the flurry of speculation going on among the Laundry Club Ladies and them pecking the situation like chickens feeding, I slipped away to the office. I was sure they didn't even notice.

They were too wrapped up with the image of Henry Bryant in the back of Hank's sheriff's car and doing too much speculating to even see me walk away.

The office was the first building as soon as you drove into the long drive up the entrance of Happy Trails Campground—and right in front of the recreation building and tiki bar—so I had a good view of Abby's party while I made a phone call down to Agnes Swift.

"I was wondering when you were going to give me a call. Now, I know it's probably not to check on me since, well"—her voice cracked —"I can't even bring myself to say it without crying."

"Oh, Agnes, you're going to make me cry." When I called Agnes at the sheriff's department, my sole focus was to ask her why Henry was being hauled down to the station, and I'd never figured on having to talk about what had taken place with me and Hank.

Especially since she was Hank's granny.

"I told that boy that he didn't need to worry about the mule going blind. Just load the wagon." Agnes was all sorts of serious, but it gave me a good chuckle, breaking up the lump in my throat.

"Agnes, I don't think he is going to change his mind about kids. I know you mean well and that it was your way of telling him he's nothing like how his father was a father to him and creating a home with me would change his mind, but it's something he's going to have to come to grips with, not you telling him." For a second, I felt like I'd actually grown up a smidgen and actually understood where Hank had been coming from. "But that's not why I called."

"I know. I know," she resumed, making my stomach settle, in the hope we were moving forward. "You're calling about Henry Bryant. I told Hank you were having Abby's send-off today and not to disturb Henry, but you know Hank. He's got that badge stuck on his hip like he's something. I told him he was getting too big for his britches."

There was a buzz on her end of the line.

"Oops. Hold on, Mae." There was some clicking in the background. "Normal's dispatch, how can I help you?"

"It's still me." I smiled, picturing her all flustered over the situation with Hank. Agnes had actually raised Hank into the man he was today, and she loved him so much. There was no doubt in my mind she was just as devastated as me and Hank.

Hank and I could've gone on like we were, but it was better to address the issues now at our age instead of later. It had come as a big shock to our small Southern community, and I was not spared from idle gossip.

My skin had gotten thick over the years from being the center of speculation and finger-pointing. It just seemed like a walk in the park these days. But my heart hadn't hardened, and there was an inkling of hope Hank would come around to the idea of having children.

If I couldn't hold on to hope, I wasn't sure my heart would be able to host this amazing wedding and union between two people I dearly loved.

While I waited for Agnes to hop back on the line, I walked over to the window and peeled back the curtain. Abby had come out of the

Pamper Camper. I didn't see Mary Elizabeth or Betts, so I assumed Mary Elizabeth had gone into the Pamper Camper while Betts was with Tex, doing the reiki.

Abby, Dawn, and Queenie were sitting down at the table, enjoying some of the food Ty Randal had catered from his diner, the Normal Diner.

"Mae, you there?" Agnes asked.

"I am."

"I've got to hurry up because it was Hank and he asked me to get some food for Henry." The familiar sound of a squeaky chair from her end was a sure sign she was getting up. "From what I understand, there's been a report Henry has been doing some illegal logging, and you know we don't fool around with that kind of nonsense."

Illegal logging was not tolerated in the national forests, and it came with a hefty prison sentence, not to mention a fine if found guilty.

"Why on earth do they think Henry would do something like that?" I asked.

"The forest rangers had been out on one of their runs to check the logging report and if the harvesting had been completed."

The logging report was the official document that contained all of the loggers who had been cleared to harvest. Timber logging, if done correctly, was actually healthy for the forest and the improved wildlife habitat as well as reducing the risk of forest fires, which was another issue we had locally.

"The rangers went out to check their blue marks and found some trees harvested that weren't marked." Agnes was talking about how the rangers would mark the trees that were to be removed, with blue spray paint. "They had put up some cameras to make sure the work was done properly. When they went back to see who took down the trees that weren't approved, there was Henry, ax and all, sawing away."

"I just don't think Henry would do such a thing." My shoulders slumped as I even tried to wrap my head around such an accusation.

"Yep. I thought the same thing, too, but I seen it with my own eyes. Now, granted, my eyes are old like me, but they can still make out people I know." She let out a long sigh. "You should know about the Timberwood Project."

"The Timberwood Project?" I asked for clarification.

"Yep. The National Parks Committee project that you helped vote through." She reminded me of the latest issue I had with sitting on the board of the National Parks Committee.

The project had been brought to us by the rangers with their partnership with Environmental Group for Animal Habitats last summer. If there was one thing I was passionate about, it was the animals and the forest, as well as the trees. So when the rangers brought us this project that not only helped our local forest but also gave a place for the local children to go for a camp and to learn about the community they lived in, I was interested.

It wasn't all hippie-dippie "save the trees" and tree huggers—it was actually about strategically logging the trees so that the forest could flourish and thrive, two very different things.

"The project has started?" I asked, not realizing the final document had been signed off by Executive Judge Gab Hemmer, the person who also sat on the board to sign off on the project.

"I've got the paperwork right here. He signed off on it three weeks ago. The first round of logging was a week ago, and well, that's when the rangers went out to see it before they could go to the next phase." I didn't like the tone of Agnes's voice. "Mae, I think he's in a little bit of a pickle."

There was a little bit of noise in the background.

"Oops. They're here, and I don't have the bologna sandwich made. I sure wish you and my grandson would make up." She didn't even wait for me to respond, which I was sure was on purpose, before she hung up the phone.

Abby's laughter spilled into the office. I looked out the window and saw Bobby Ray had stopped by.

There was no way I was going to be able to let them keep Henry in jail overnight. By law, they could keep him for twenty-four hours for questioning. The wedding was in under fifteen hours, and I needed Henry there to help out.

I headed over to my desk and shuffled through some of the files and meeting notes I personally had for my part of the committee. Since we met at the National Parks Office and seeing it was late on Friday night, I knew no one would be there for me to call to see if I could get the report the rangers and the Environmental of Animal Habitats had drawn up, so I had to rely on my memory and the lack of notes I'd taken a few months ago.

"This is data from three years." I read my notes out loud after I'd found them. "The purpose of the science-based plan is for restoration and recovery of large areas of old growth."

I remembered them saying that by taking down some of the trees, we'd be able to log the timber as well as thin out these particular parts, which helped not only the growth of the natural habitat of plants and foliage, but would cut back on wildfires, which saved animal habitats.

"It's the rangers who want to log the trees and the environmental group who want to see the habitats restored." I had flipped the notebook sideways to read the note I'd written, which was how I would document my opinion on matters.

It was clear it was the rangers who wanted more logging than the environmental group, but in the end, it appeared as if they came together to work a proposal we had ultimately passed.

I reached over and grabbed a sticky note.

"Check to see if the rangers and the environmental group had filed separate proposals before they presented this one." I'd written it down before I smacked it on top of the notes I'd taken a few months ago.

One thing I had learned right off the bat when I accepted the appointed position on the board was that I wouldn't put it past anyone when it came to getting something they wanted. It was very well documented by the Normal Gazette and the sheriff's department how the Environmental Group for Animal Habitats had several rallies.

A few years ago, I remembered, they'd lain down in front of some of the blacktop trucks after Mayor Courtney Mackenzie had gotten some government money to repair some much-needed park roads. The environmental group didn't even want that to happen.

Then there were the rangers. They'd spent a lot of their time trying to get the environmental groups to stop squatting on the land and protesting. It was virtually impossible for them to get the logging the forest needed to thrive.

It was such a tug and pull, both very important tasks and both equally important for the future of the Daniel Boone National Forest, but which side had Henry Bryant gotten caught up in?

That was my question. The only way I knew it was going to get answered was to actually go see him so that I could somehow use that to get him out of jail before the wedding.

But how?

"What are you doing here?" I questioned Bobby Ray before I gave him a big hug after I ventured back over to the party.

"I thought I'd come give my bride one last goodbye kiss before I head over to Hank's." Abruptly, Bobby Ray stiffened and clamped his mouth shut.

"It's okay. Come to think of it, it's great." I could feel the tension between my friends as if they had to keep it a secret that they still talked to Hank. "I'm glad you and Hank are still friends. Heck, I'm still friends with him. What's he got planned?"

"Just guy stuff. You know. I'd never have asked him to be my best man if I'd known y'all were going to break up." Bobby Ray rubbed a hand over his thinning hair before he dug both of them into the pockets of his jeans.

It was nice to see him in something other than grease-covered mechanic overalls.

"Bobby Ray, stop it." I put my hand on his arm. "It's no big deal. Honest." I moved my hands over my heart. "He is a good guy. I'm glad you have him."

"You better tell him that he better get Henry Bryant back here before your wedding, or else I'll be giving him a piece of my mind."

Mary Elizabeth brushed her hand along Bobby Ray's shoulder, cleaning him up.

For a hot second, I wondered if she was going to spit in her hand and brush his hair back like she used to do when we were kids.

Bobby Ray's phone rang. He pulled it out of his pocket to see who it was. Mary Elizabeth kept talking.

"Now, go on and say goodbye to Abby. You two lovebirds are going to have to wait until tomorrow to see each other. Did you hear me, Bobby Ray?"

"Yeah. I've got to take this." He put a finger in the air, stepping away to take the call.

"Who do you reckon that is?" Dottie asked.

I wrapped my arms around my body as Dottie lit up a cigarette. There was a sudden chill to this warm summer night, a chill I knew all too well—the kind not from a sudden breeze or drop in temperatures, but one that told me something wasn't right.

When Bobby Ray turned around, a weird feeling of dread crawled through me.

"Maybelline, can I talk to you for a second?" He called me over with a jerk of his head.

"Hmm." Dottie's brows rose. She crossed one arm under the other and held her cigarette out, away from her body.

Bobby Ray's lips trembled underneath the fake smile.

"I'm going to keep smiling and talking so they don't think anything is wrong, but that was Henry. He said he's been trying to call you because he's in trouble and needs you to come down to the sheriff's department."

I patted around my body.

"Shoot. I bet I left my phone in the office. What's going on?" I asked.

"He said they have him on video for illegal logging, and Hank just told him that he's going to charge him. Henry said he wanted his one phone call. I just got it." His voice was tight as he talked. "Not that I think he did anything wrong, but this is certainly not a good time to be arrested. I'm not trying to be insensitive, but he was going to help me move all the tables and chairs for the wedding and reception in the morning."

"You're not being insensitive. It's your wedding, and this does put a little bind on things. I'll take care of the tables and chairs." Here I was again, promising things I had no clue how I would pull off with such short notice, though I had ideas.

"I'm guessing Hank is going to be late to my party." Bobby Ray curled his lips, and his nostrils grew as he took a big inhale. "Do you think I need to postpone the wedding?"

"Absolutely not. You probably should tell Abby what is going on." My suggestion was met with a gaping mouth, narrowed eyes, and drooping brows. "Or not."

He made the dumbest suggestion. "I think you can tell her something."

"What do you want me to tell her?" I shifted my eyes to the side, gesturing toward the beady eyes focusing on us, all the Laundry Club Ladies.

Bobby Ray gave me no help. "I don't know. Make something up. You're good at that. When can you go see Henry? Maybe you can get him out of jail."

"I don't think I have that kind of pull anymore." Not that I'd had much say in things before, but at least I was able to get in front of Hank when I needed a favor. Right now, there was no way he was going to give me a moment of face time.

Despite what I'd been telling my family and friends, even Agnes, about my current relationship with Hank, friendly it wasn't. I'd seen him out and about in town, even at the diner, but he didn't even look my way. It was something I thought would go away with some time and probably would, but time wasn't on our side at this particular moment.

I needed to figure something out, and fast. But I wasn't sure when I could get away from the party I was giving Abby at the moment.

"Bobby!" Abby called him over.

"Look"—he put his hand out—"I don't want Abby knowing anything about this."

"They all saw Hank take Henry out of here."

"You tell them he was taking him to the party so he could have some adult beverage or something." He looked at me under his brows. "After what happened to Abby's engagement ring, you owe this to me."

He left me standing there just as Tex called me over.

On my way over to Tex, I overheard Bobby Ray say to Abby, "I sure wish I didn't have to rush off, but if you and me are getting hitched, then I've got to go."

Tex patted the table for me to jump up on and instructed me to lie down.

"Hmmm." Tex's hands waved over me. "You've depleted your emotions."

He had his eyes closed.

"You've given your emotions away today, and not your happy ones." When he said that, I squinted, and he was looking at me. "Are you going to tell me, or do I have to do this blindly?" He paused and noticed my silence. "Fine."

He took his levitating hands from over me and bent down to get something from his bag. He stood up with a white towel and placed it over my eyes.

"Your frequency ribbons are off."

I recalled him telling me about how to think of ribbons above my head when I'd first met him. These different-colored ribbons of high frequencies included things like emotions, abundance, happiness, and joy.

"Your unhealthy ribbons are taking over with their low frequency, and we need to get those removed before the big day tomorrow. Since it doesn't appear as if you're going to tell me what is going on so I can pinpoint how to help you, I'm going to work on your balance. You need to balance all of your emotions to get you through the event." He did soothe me somewhat when he didn't press me for what I was tense about.

That soon passed, because the next thing he wanted to know was if I was worried about seeing Hank.

"Yes. No. Yes. No." I teetered back and forth. "Of course I am, but that's not why I'm tense." I pulled the towel off of my eyes and sat up. "Henry Bryant is in jail, about to be booked on charges of illegal logging. He isn't going to be able to help out tomorrow like Mary Elizabeth had hired him to do, and normally, I'd try to get Hank to let him off for a few hours, but with this whole taking-a-break thing, I can't just call him up and give him a wink and a smile and ask for a favor."

Tex stepped back.

"Why not?" Tex asked. "You know him and his reactions to most things by now. Just because the two of you broke up doesn't mean you can't work together for the greater good."

He gestured for me to flip over onto my stomach.

"I guess what I'm saying is maybe if you two didn't focus on each other as much, which I'm assuming you didn't do in the beginning of the relationship, but focus on the greater good"—he laid his warm hands on my shoulders—"then you could possibly figure out what brought the two of you together and see if whatever it was that broke you apart is fixable, manageable, or even compromisable, if that's a word." He laughed and left me with some things to gnaw on.

He was right. Hank and I had had a great relationship in the beginning. Though I didn't see us compromising on the issue of children, I could see where I was valuable to him when it came to checking things out like I did in his past cases.

CHAPTER FOUR

"I really shouldn't be eating these ribs. The sodium alone will make me balloon up." Abby Fawn had no reason to worry about blowing up.

"Be sure to drink you some good ol'-fashion water." Queenie was all things exercise and good nutrition. She never had anyone diet, but she sure did give advice on what was healthy for your body and what wasn't.

She was always on Dottie for smoking.

Betts, Queenie, and Abby continued their conversation, while Mary Elizabeth and Dawn started to clear the table to make way for the dessert Christine Watson, owner of the Cookie Crumble Bakery, had gifted Abby for the night-before event.

When I saw the two-tiered cake, I knew it was all Mary Elizabeth's doing. It had Southern-bride vibes emanating from it. The top tier was a quilted pattern in a pale-green fondant. The bottom tier was larger in circumference, covered with white fondant but decorated with what we Southerners called the blue Southern rose pattern, but in this case, it was done in the same pale-green fondant as the top tier.

Nothing in Abby's life ever had a Southern stamp, but the reaction she was giving them was a genuine love for the dessert.

"What's goin' on in that head of yours?" Dottie ambled up to me with a cigarette in hand.

"You know." I rolled my eyes. "The usual. How on earth am I going to help Henry since he's been hauled down to the department for illegal logging? Apparently."

"That's what Hank Sharp has his knickers in a wad about?" Dottie's eyes lowered. "He's got some kinda nerve to do this to Abby right before her wedding. I bet it's just some sort of excuse to see you today because you know as well as I do that it could've waited. My goodness, Richard Mitchell has been illegally loggin' all his life, and I've never once seen him shoved in the back of a sheriff's car."

"Any relation to Shannon?" I asked about the waitress down at the Normal Diner.

We didn't know a lot about Shannon. She had taken the job after a much-beloved member of the diner family died, and well, I just hadn't taken the time to get to know Shannon. It felt like a betrayal in some ways to my friend who passed, and that seemed to be an issue with me —loyalty.

It was something I'd taken pride in when I was younger, but now that I was in my thirties, I was seeing it'd done more harm than good. I just wasn't so sure I would be able to change my ways, but I guessed just talking to Shannon would be a first step in the right direction even if I would be fishing for some information on logging.

"Yep. They are cousins. But they all live in a family compound down off Belcher Bog." Dottie rolled words off her tongue so fast I couldn't keep up. "By the look on your face, I'm guessin' you don't know where that's at."

My brows jumped up, and my eyes opened wide. "I don't even know what you just said."

"You're gonna go out of the campground and turn left. After you get out of town"—she meant downtown Normal, that I did know—"you're gonna take that sharp turn by the barn with the faded quilt on the side. That belongs to Helen Pyle's people. They need to repaint that old barn or tear that sucker down." She took a long drag off her cigarette before she went back to giving me directions to Belcher Bog.

"Anyhow, once you take that hairpin turn, you keep on going 'bout two or so miles, and you'll come upon three rocks 'bout the size of your car. You can't miss 'em. There, you'll take a left and go about three-fourths a way down that rock wall before you get to a left turn. That's Belcher Bog. It's a little Appalachian community, but really, just the Mitchells all took over down there. I'm not even sure if anyone that's not a Mitchell lives down yonder now."

I didn't care about all of that. I just wanted to see Shannon and possibly get some information from her or her cousin about logging and all the details or laws behind it.

I had access to the Timberwood Project proposal from the rangers and the Environmental Group for Animal Habitats, but I didn't truly understand what all of it meant. I had relied on Judge Executive Hemmer and Lloyd Hornbuckle to give me the insight so I could make the best decision I could when it was brought forth to the committee.

"My first guess would be to see if you can get Henry out of jail." Dottie made a good point. "And by the way, the moon is popping up over the trees. I'm figuring you ain't got much time to get down there and bail him out."

"Yeah. I thought about that, but then I was giving Hank some time to bring him back."

"If you do go down there, I suggest you comb that hair. You look like you've been running around like a chicken being chased by Colonel Sanders." She took a long draw and leaned back, blowing smoke rings up in the air.

"Thank you, Dottie." I looked back over at the ladies cutting the cake.

"Don't you give them any thought. I'll keep 'em entertained 'til you get back." There was no doubt in my mind that Dottie would do that. Just watching her was enough entertainment for hours, especially when she tried to do something to keep your attention. "And I reckon you oughtta call in some help for tomorrow if he ain't gettin' out of jail. I'll take care of Fifi."

I shook my head and slipped away into the dusk.

When I got my car and drove past our little bridal party, I didn't see any of them turn to notice me. They were still eating and laughing, which was exactly how I wanted Abby to feel and look the day before her special day, which made me feel so much better that I had slipped away.

"Judge," I said out loud after I called Judge Hemmer on my way over to the jail, "I'm sorry it's so late."

"That's all right, Mae. Is something wrong?" he asked.

"Well, I'm not sure, but Henry Bryant has been taken down to the jail on charges of illegal logging. I know we had that proposal go through, but did you hear of any illegal logging?" I asked.

"Nah. I was down at Helen Pyle's place, getting my hair cut so I could look presentable for the big day tomorrow, and I did hear Helen say her cousin Tucker had been marking up the trees. I didn't even know Harlan had moved ranger posts, but from what Helen was telling someone, he's here doing the work for the proposal we pushed through."

"So in other words, I could ask Helen if she can get me in contact with Tucker?" I asked after listening to Judge Hemmer yammer on about how these people were related.

"I reckon you can. I'm sure she'd get you in touch with him. How is this going to help Henry?" he asked.

"Henry said he was hired by someone to cut down some trees, and I'm going down to the station now to see him, so I'm hoping to have someone's name. That proposal has a lot of names on there for the logging, and I wanted to see if whoever hired him is on the proposal. If so, then maybe Henry accidentally cut down some trees that possibly Tucker accidentally marked." I wondered if Tucker just didn't know the area or have the right plat for the job since he was new to this ranger's post.

"I'm not sure if rangers get things wrong, but I guess it's possible. Henry will still have a pretty hefty fine."

I wasn't so sure about that. If I could prove somehow the tree that Henry took down was marked for logging, then whoever marked the tree would be responsible for the fines, then Henry would be off the hook.

That was it! I could definitely find the person who hired him and go from there. Henry would be back at Happy Trails way before the wedding.

CHAPTER FIVE

The sheriff's department was located in the business district. They actually didn't have their own free-standing building but occupied a portion of the courthouse, which Mayor Mackenzie had been trying to get moved so she could make more space for the county clerk and circuit clerk since Normal had grown in population and the lines for property taxes, as well as car taxes, had gotten longer.

Now that Hank and I were no longer an official item, I wasn't getting the rundown on where that internal battle stood.

The business district was located past the downtown area, and when I drove through downtown, I noticed a lot of tourists were still out and about.

Normal was one of those cozy Southern towns that hosted charming festivals, quaint streets, and a downtown that wrapped you up like a snuggly hug. It was one of those towns that someone who discovered it always came back to.

The people milling around downtown were the incentive I used to make Happy Trails Campground what it was today. In my mind, I had all the coziness of the grassy median that was located on the one-way Main Street. The median was a little swatch of wooded paradise like the woods around the campground. The large oak trees in the grassy area were no different from the large oaks around Happy Trails. There was an amphitheater and covered seating area in the median that I used as an example for the recreation center and tiki bar.

Using the idea of the twinkling lights wrapped around all the street carriage lights and hanging all over the tree trunks and amphitheater pillars, I'd had Henry string lights all over the campground.

It just made everything seem so romantic, cozy, and personal. I loved the feeling it gave me when I was downtown, so I knew my guests would love it too. Thick white pillars you'd see on the front porch of a plantation home held up the structure. Each post had a real gas lantern hanging off it. Large ferns toppled over several ceramic planters. There were twinkling lights around each pole, giving it such a romantic feel.

I had even incorporated the small shop along Main Street as part of my marketing plan. For instance, Smelly Dog, which was a pet groomer, had coupons off for my guests to get anything they needed for their pets while camping. Normal Diner gave me coupons to hand out to my guests for a buy-one-get-one meal.

The Tough Nickel Thrift Shop and Deter's Feed-N-Seed, along with more boutique-type shops, also gave coupons to get a percentage off or even a free local decal. Campers loved stickers of the places they'd been, to put on their camping gear.

So I worked really hard to get my name out by partnering with these downtown shops.

There was no better time than summertime to visit the Daniel Boone National Park, and all the shops had displays to welcome them.

The community had really preserved all the small cottage-style homes by turning the area into shops. Just like a home, each shop had its own swatch of land, which created like a small courtyard between the stores.

Today, those courtyards were filled with tourists, and late at night too. Summer was in full swing.

But my eyes were set on driving out of downtown on my way to the business district, where I was on a mission to get Henry out of jail before it was completely dark outside.

"Can't do it." Al Hemmer's thumbs were tucked in the pockets of his brown sheriff's pants. He rocked back on the heels of his cowboy boots. "No can do, Mae. Until I hear from Sheriff Sharp, Henry Bryant stays in that cell."

"Has he been formally charged?" I asked.

Al didn't even let me inside the walls of the department, where I would've just walked past him and down the hall and found Henry myself. Nope, I stood in the entryway. He talked to me through the sliding window where Agnes Swift sat on the opposite side to monitor the riffraff that came in before they opened the actual door to step inside.

"Mae." Al gave me a stern look. He was fairly new as a sheriff's deputy, and unfortunately for me, he played by all the rules—no exceptions.

Give him time, I thought to myself.

"I was told specifically if you came down here not to let you see him."

"Al, I'm hurt." I lifted my hands to my chest. "Do y'all think I'm a threat to the department? Little ol' me?" I batted my eyes.

"Now, don't you be making eyes at me now that you're single. Hank told me you'd pull out all the stops to get Henry out of jail." Al wasn't budging.

"Wow." I shrugged. "I guess Hank Sharp is scared of me. All five foot five of me?"

And to think I'd actually done what Dottie told me to do and fixed my unruly curly hair just in case I ran into Hank.

"Well." Al shuffled his feet. "I guess when you put it that way, I'm not sure what you could do if you stood outside of the cell."

Al looked over his shoulder then slowly slid his gaze back to me. A long sigh escaped him.

"I reckon you can come in for one minute." He held up a finger.

A smile crossed my lips. There was a buzz at the door. I grabbed the handle before he could change his mind and took off across the floor of the department, where all of their desks were located.

"Wait a minute, Mae." Al tried to keep up with me as I hurried down the hall. "I knew I shouldn't've let you in."

"Henry?" I called and looked in the windows on each side of the hall into the interrogation rooms in case he was in there, with a little giddyup in my step. "Henry?" I called out.

"Honestly, Mae. Please stop." Al groaned. "Dagnabbit. I'm gonna call Hank."

"Call him!" I yelled over my shoulder and was relieved to see Henry sitting in the last interrogation room at the table with a cup of coffee.

I opened the door.

"Mae, are you taking me home?" There was a look of relief on Henry's face.

"I don't know." I hurried over to him and gave him a hug. "I'll do my best. But we have to talk fast. Al is calling Hank, so I'm sure I don't have much time with you."

Henry smiled.

"So tell me about this man you were doing work for. Do you have a name?" I asked.

"Yep." Henry nodded. "His name is Duke Weaver. He stopped by the campground a few weeks ago, and Dottie was there. She can tell ya."

I rolled my hand to gesture him to keep talking, signaling the importance of time and that we needed to hurry.

"How many weeks ago?" I was trying to decide if the timing was along the same timeline as the proposal.

"I reckon a few." *A few* was actually a time, according to people in Normal.

"I'm looking for specifics. Like two weeks? Three?" I had to nail it down.

"We'll just go in the middle and say two and a half weeks. Is that good?" he asked.

I nodded, knowing I wasn't going to get a specific nailed-down time.

"And, well, he said he owned some property on the edge of the forest and he wanted to get some trees cut down. Something about being part of the Environmental Group for Animal Habitat, you know, the group

Violet Rhinehammer interviewed on the television show. It was two big oaks, and well, you know me. I like to keep busy, and I like to have some extra money for the hard winters. I took it, figuring it was part of the logging contract with the National Parks too. You're on the committee. You know about it."

"And his name is Duke Weaver?" I asked to be sure I heard him right.

"Mmhh. Duke Weaver. I remember because I love the Duke—you know, John Wayne, the Duke. I love to watch them old westerns. There was one on tonight I was going to watch on the public television channel. I reckon I done missed the beginning, but I can catch the end if you get me out of here."

"Duke Weaver," I said the name out loud then repeated it in my head so I didn't forget. "And this guy, did you get paid?"

"Nope. Not a penny. I told him I'd be back to get the money, and he told me he'd meet me at the Normal Diner with my cash. I went there a few days after I got them trees down, and nothing." Henry looked down at his hands. "He mentioned getting the money from the Timberwood Project."

"Timberwood Project?" I knew it. Those environmentalists would stop at nothing to get what they wanted when it wasn't in the best interest of the whole. I'd bet they were behind this illegal logging just so they could stop some of the other projects the park had on tap that didn't fit in with their needs. "When did you go to the diner?" I asked.

"Tuesdee." He nodded.

"This past Tuesday?" I asked. He nodded again.

"Did you see anyone at the diner that can say you were there?"

"Yep. I got me a slice of Kentucky bourbon pie." He licked his lips. "That goes fast when it's on the menu. Ty told me he would save me a slice." He grinned. "He did too."

"You talked to Ty?" I asked to make sure because Ty was a very upstanding citizen and maybe he knew this Duke Weaver.

"I did. He even gave it to me for free since I put some extra firewood on his woodpile next to his camper." Henry leaned back, pushed his chair back from the table, and stood up. "Can we leave now?"

Hank opened the door. "Not so fast."

I had the urge to scream and tell my heart to stop the dropping sensation that made my stomach feel like I was going to puke after coming face-to-face with Hank Sharp for the first time since we'd ended it.

CHAPTER SIX

"Mae, I knew you'd come here." Hank stomped his foot and jerked away from me so I couldn't see his face. "I'm gonna discipline Al. I gave him orders not to let you in."

"Don't do that. It's my fault. I talked him into letting me see Henry."

I knew my words hit Hank, not because I could see his face—I couldn't—but how he tightened his fists told me he was trying not to yell at me.

"I have to help him." There was nothing in the words I said that should've surprised Hank.

"Of course you do. That's another big problem we have," he muttered under his breath though I heard them clearly.

"What did you say?" I asked.

He turned around. There was a hard look in his green eyes I'd never seen. Something told me that standing in front of him made him more angry than what I'd done with Al.

Hank lied to me for the first time ever. "I said you can leave. Henry isn't going anywhere. There's a warrant out for his arrest from the rangers, and there's nothing I can do about it."

"A warrant?" My jaw dropped, my head tilted.

"Don't look at me like that. It's a warrant. He is seen on the video footage from the cameras the rangers put out when there's a logging so people don't cut down trees that aren't allowed. In this case, it's strong. It's Henry, and he admitted to cutting them down—two huge, healthy oaks that have to be hundreds of years old."

"Did you check into this Duke Weaver guy?" I asked Hank.

"He's on the list to go see tomorrow after the wedding. It's too late tonight, and I've got the right to hold Henry." His chest filled with a huge inhale. "There's nothing you can do but go home."

"I don't believe that, Hank Sharp. I think you can do something about it. And I want it done." I had to think for a second.

My usual go-to phone call was Ava Cox, but she was currently out of town for some lawyer convention. There weren't any good attorneys locally that would fight to get Henry out tonight. I appeared to have my hands tied for the first time with Hank.

Ever.

"Did you go through your little routine in your head? It's not going to work this time. Henry Bryant did what he did, and he's been arrested for it. Now, on Monday, he will go before the judge to set bail money. Then you can call Granny, Agnes"—I glowered at him when he called her Agnes, making this so professional—"and she will take the bond money from you. You will get a receipt, and then he's in your hands until trial. He will be found guilty."

"You need to arrest Duke Weaver for telling him the wrong trees." I was about to throw a big-sized hissy fit.

What was it Tex had told me to help that layer of ribbons? Desperately, I tried to remember, but instead, I pictured cutting those ribbons to shreds.

"Mae, I know that look on your face, so before you get all up in a tizzy, I am telling you that I'm not going to let him go into your custody or Ava's custody. I'm seeing this through. This is a very important matter to not only the Rangers, but to our community and the life of the Daniel Boone National Forest." He was solid on his stance.

My jaw clenched. I tried to breathe so the blood pumping through my heart would get enough oxygen to stop the skipping beats.

"Hank." My voice lowered. My shoulders fell. "Please don't hold him because of us."

He grinned and shook his head.

"I knew you'd think that. But don't be so full of yourself, Mae. This is a federal offense, and no matter what the status between us is or was, it has nothing to do with you."

And there he did it. He put me in my place just like that.

"I'm sorry you feel that way. But can you find it in the kindness of your heart to just give me the paperwork instead of me going through the online files to pull everything I need?" I asked.

"When his lawyer gets back in town, I will forward those to her." He was in some way letting me know that Ava had been contacted.

"Can I go say goodbye to him? He has no one."

With his mouth slightly open, his tongue played with his teeth, jutting his jaw to the side before he let his gaze fall to my face.

"Please?"

"Fine. Goodbye, and that's it," he warned and hit a button on the phone. "Al, let Mae say goodbye to Henry. One minute. That's it." Hank threw a finger at the door. "Al is waiting."

"Thanks, Hank." I knew I had to play nice, and I knew no matter what he was saying, he was holding this over my head.

I didn't know how I was going to do it, but I was going to get my way. Henry might not get out tonight. But I could guarantee he'd be out by that time tomorrow.

CHAPTER SEVEN

I t was good and dark by the time I made it back to Happy Trails Campground, but that didn't stop the Laundry Club Ladies from partying. Life flickered out of the campfires across the campground and reminded me how life around me was still happening. More fires going meant more wood needed to be delivered. If Henry wasn't here, who was going to do it until he got back?

Slowly, I drove to my campsite and parked my little car on the concrete pad in front of my camper van, which I rarely took out of its spot. It was easier to have a little Ford Focus to get around in when I needed to go to town instead of not only unplugging from all the amenities but securing everything inside of my home on wheels so they didn't fall off or out and break on impact.

With my phone in my hand, I nibbled on my bottom lip and sucked in a deep breath. I scrolled through my contacts and hit the text-message button when I got to Beck Greer's phone number.

Me: Hey, Beck. It's Mae from Happy Trails. I'm not sure what you're doing this summer, but I'd love it if you could work here. I'm more than happy to pick you up and bring you home every day. Please talk it over with your mama and let me know. Also, if you could start tomorrow, that'd be great. Please let me know ASAP.

Beck was Ava's ten-year-old neighbor, who had given me his business card when I was visiting Ava. He called himself the Mow Monster, and I had used him at the campground for various odd jobs like weeding and possibly snooping. Not that I used him to snoop—he just knew everything about everyone. He was the product of listening to his mama and her friends gossip so much.

Outside of him spilling his guts about everything he knew, he was a hard worker, and I actually trusted him to do the odd jobs around here that Henry did on a daily basis, one of those being delivering wood to the campers every single day.

My phone chirped back.

Beck: Yes. My mama said that'd be fine and she would bring me and pick me up herself. I can start tomorrow at eight a.m.

I sent back a thumbs-up emoji to let him know I had gotten it and eight in the morning was fine. I got out of my car so that I could get Fifi out for a potty break before I headed over to the bungalow to finish out the night with some of those cheap spa masks Dottie had gotten down at the Safeway grocery store for a buck each. I hoped it didn't break us all out, but I would do anything for Abby, and if it meant getting a pimple the size of a basketball on the tip of my nose, I was going to do it.

The light of campfires was probably enough to keep any sort of coyotes or bears away, but I didn't want to take a chance with the possibility, so I put Fifi on her leash and took a long stroll around the lake.

I smiled and greeted the campers who were still outside. Sounds of laughter, chatter, singing, and a little yelling drifted along the breeze as it trilled across the overturned canoes on the beach and rippled over the lake. My mind turned to Henry and thoughts of him sitting in the cell with his head down, defeated.

It was the way he looked when I left him, and my heart ached to think such a wonderful and kind man could do what they'd said he'd done. Sure, he admitted to cutting down the trees. He was hired to do it, and I didn't understand why on earth Hank had not decided to stop by there tomorrow.

"What's going on up there?" Abby Fawn was sitting in an Adirondack chair on the dock.

Fifi heard Abby's voice and darted that way, pulling the leash taut.

"Hey. I didn't see you there." I stumbled over as fast as I could without Fifi choking herself. "You okay?"

"Yeah. I'm good. The ladies were getting a little rowdy in the bungalow, and I called Bobby Ray to see what they were doing. Hank got a poker game together, and from the sound of it, Tucker Pyle is taking them to the cleaners."

"Tucker Pyle, huh." I snarled.

"I'm guessing you've met the new ranger." Abby giggled.

"Nope. Not yet. I plan on it after this wedding." I sat down on the dock. I brought my knees up to my chest and wrapped my arms around my legs with Fifi's leash around my wrist.

"Henry?" Abby glanced over. The moon caught her side profile.

"How did you know?" I asked.

"Are you kidding? I saw what happened with Hank, then I noticed you were gone." The sound of snapping twigs echoed from the woods behind us. "I know you very well. So tell me what happened at the department."

"I'm not going to tell you the night before your wedding." The whine of a few rickety camper air conditioners came to life. The humidity was settling in, and my naturally curly hair was going to look like springs in any photos for the wedding.

Now, I wished I did have a hair appointment with Helen Pyle at Cute-icles because she would definitely have the lowdown on her cousin and how I could go about talking to him about the Henry situation.

"I've got some help coming tomorrow, to get the wedding all set up, so don't you worry that sweet head of yours. You are going to become my sister tomorrow, and nothing is going to ruin it," I assured her.

"I do understand if you need to go check something out." She gave me the side-eye like she knew something was going on. "Or you can tell me what you know, and I can help a little before I go off on my honeymoon."

I was so excited for her and Bobby Ray to finally get away on a trip out of here. Both of them were going to jet off someplace warm and tropical, sip on fruity drinks, and put their toes in the warm sand.

"Henry is in a bit of a pickle. He said someone hired him to cut down some trees for the Timberwood Project, and apparently these trees weren't to be logged. This man, Duke Weaver, hired him. I told Hank to go see this man and arrest him, but he said it was too late."

"Duke Weaver? He came into the library, asking me if I knew a handyman. I gave him Henry's number. I had no idea he is with that environmental group." Abby blinked a few times. Her forehead wrinkled, her jaw set. "He never even mentioned it."

"When was this?" I asked out of habit as a timeline of events started to unfold in my head.

"It was two weeks ago tomorrow. I remember because it was late and the gals at the library were giving me a small wedding shower after hours at the library. When he came in, I clearly remember thinking that this guy was going to take forever." She laughed. "I can always peg people who come into the library who have never stepped foot in a library. Those are the ones I have to take time to show around and pretty much find what they are looking for."

Fifi lay down on the dock.

"But if you need to go and do something tonight for Henry"—Abby turned and looked at me—"I'm fine with it. Life doesn't stop because I'm getting married."

She was so sweet.

"You know what?" I clasped my hands together and put them between my knees. "I don't need to leave. Hank has Henry all situated at the department. I'm sure Al Hemmer is there to make sure Henry's needs are met throughout the night. He's fine for now. There's no way I can get the judge to set bail tonight anyways."

I left out the part where Hank was going to wait until a bail hearing on Monday for Henry. I knew the judge would be able to issue one tomorrow, but it was Saturday, the day of the wedding, and all the people, including the judges, who would be able to set Henry's bail were going to be at the Milkery, watching Abby and Bobby Ray get hitched.

This meant Henry was probably going to be staying in jail until Monday, and I had to look at it as time.

Time for me to get Henry's timeline established and time to get me Duke Weaver's personal information so that I could pay the man a visit of my own.

Unfortunately, I had a feeling it wasn't going to be as easy as I thought.

CHAPTER EIGHT

The thing with a small Southern town—people were able to put their differences aside and come together when someone needed help. When I showed up at the Milkery ready to pull the old tables out of the Milkery's office for the wedding and reception, I was surprised when Bobby Ray, Hank, Ty, Buck, Alvin Deters, and Joel Grassel had already gotten everything set up and all I had to do was help Mary Elizabeth cloak everything in white linens before Jessica Niles from the Sweet Smell Flower Shop showed up to make it the magical fairy wedding Abby wanted.

And by "fairy wedding," I meant romantic feeling, lights dangling from the trees, moss-type flower arrangements dangling all over the tents, as well as little fairy gardens on a few pieces of wood stumps Bobby Ray had found somewhere.

Abby loved to read fantasy novels, and she had been following a new author's romances that included paranormal elements. She'd been trying to get our book club to read one, but it wasn't a genre Dottie or Mary Elizabeth was into.

The group of men were standing over by the tent, drinking coffee and looking a little rough. No doubt, they'd all had too much to drink and little sleep before they got here. Another thing about this group of men—they took in Bobby Ray Bonds when I asked them to after Bobby Ray showed up at Happy Trails Campground when he saw an article written up about me and how I'd brought life back to the campground, which made Normal have an uptick in the economy.

Funny how I'd been trying to escape the past before I got the keys to the camper van, which drove me right back to the people I had spent so many years hiding from. Little did I realize it was those people who truly cared and loved me.

And I was grateful, though it sounded weird, that I had lost everything due to my ex-now-dead husband. Without what he did, I would never have been right here at this moment.

"You okay?" Hank had walked up to me and handed me a cup of coffee.

"Yeah. I was just looking at your group and thinking how funny life turns out." I didn't have to explain what I meant to Hank. He'd been the ear to many of the deep thoughts that I would bring to the surface during our late-night phone calls or chats around a fire.

"He's a pretty good guy. I'm happy for him and Abby." Hank glanced over at me. He brought his coffee up to his lips. The steam curled up and around his nose, shooting past his green eyes.

"I am too. Thank you for helping put all of this together this morning." It was left unsaid that if he had let Henry come with me, Hank and his buddies could've still been sleeping. "By the look of all y'all, it looks like you were up most of the night."

"Long night in Soggy Bottom, gambling and drinking." He laughed and took the last drink from his mug before he held it down to his side. "I better get going. I wanted to say hello before I took off because I know how that head of yours works, and if I didn't say goodbye, you'd come up with a million reasons why I didn't say goodbye."

"Well, thank you." I wanted to protest and tell him not to be so full of himself, but he was right. I'd beat that situation like a dead horse, throw it under a car, run over it, back up, and run over it again until I was exhausted over why he hadn't said goodbye.

"I'll see you at the wedding." He and I both knew we had big plans to go to the wedding as the maid of honor and best man.

We'd actually started writing our speeches together before the breakup and planned on making a full romantic weekend out of it. "Planned" was the key word. I'd also planned for Henry to set up the wedding venue. We were seeing how quickly plans changed.

"There you are." Mary Elizabeth rushed out of the kitchen door. It slammed behind her. "I was shocked to hear about Henry not getting out of jail." She wiped her hands down the front of her apron before she wrapped her arms around me, giving me a hug. "What on earth, Maybelline? I thought, when Hank took him out of the campground, that he'd be right back."

"Didn't we all?" I questioned. "On the bright side, everything looks like it's coming together, and the weather looks like it's going to cooperate. Where are the linens?"

"They are on hangers inside of the pantry. Betts did a wonderful job ironing them." There was no happier sight then seeing Mary Elizabeth in her element. "It's going to be beautiful." She ran her hand along my hair. "I just wish it was you."

"Okay. Enough of that." It was hard enough being here with a broken heart, much less hearing how my adoptive mama wanted to plan a big gorgeous wedding for me. "I'll get the linens out on the tables. When is Jessica getting here?"

She took her phone out of the pocket of the apron.

"Oh dear, soon." Her eyes grew. "We better get hustling because I want to make sure you have plenty of time for Helen Pyle to work on that hair of yours."

It was nice to get lost in putting all the linens on the various tables. There were round tables and long rectangle tables with several chairs around each one. I strategically placed my seat and nameplate away from Hank. Distance was the best thing I could offer myself. Well, a piece of the cake was a pretty close second. Maybe two slices.

"Over here." I waved Christine Watson over after she pulled up in her Cookie Crumble Bakery van and took out the first box, which held the bottom layer of the cake.

"How are you holding up?" she asked and set the cake on the table.

"Fine. Hank and I are on good terms." A little notch hitched in my stomach. Was this the question everyone was going to ask me today? I sure hoped not.

"No. I'm talking about Henry," she said and left the box there, walking back to her van to get more.

"Can I help you?" I asked since I wanted to hang around a few minutes longer to see what she'd heard.

"Sure."

I followed her to the van, where she had various white bakery boxes with the order they were to be placed on the cake stand written on them. "I can't believe Henry would illegally log. From what I understand, the Environmental Group of Animal Habitats didn't hire him to do the work."

"Who said that?" I asked her and took a box.

"Careful with that. Gently carry it over with one hand on the bottom. The buttercream is so heavy—I don't want the layer to fall out." She actually took her hands and corrected mine. "Violet Rhinehammer did an exclusive story on it this morning for Channel Two. She rarely works on the weekend, but today, she had Andrea Burt on there from the group. She swears they didn't have Henry do any sort of work because they had professional loggers on staff, not a simple handyman."

"In those exact words?" I wanted to know more.

"Mmhh." Christine put the cake stand on the table and opened the first box she'd brought. "We have to make sure the heat doesn't get to the cake. I know the air conditioners will help with that, and Mary Elizabeth said she'd make sure they put one near the cake."

Yeah, that was another thing Mary Elizabeth had made sure she got —portable air conditioners.

Christine and I made a couple more trips back and forth to the van before she was finally ready to assemble the best food part of the entire event.

The cake.

"What was the woman's name from the environmental group, again?" I had to keep these names straight because after this wedding, I was going to pull all the names from the proposal and thoroughly check them out.

"Andrea Burt. I should know because I'm doing the desserts for their party," she said.

"The environmental group party?"

"Yes. They had me make sugar cookies in the shape of trees and various animals in the forest to celebrate their efforts to maintain the clean environment. Didn't you get the invite? From what I heard, all the committee people are coming."

"I totally forgot about it. I was thinking I wasn't going to go because I thought I'd have my hands full with cleaning up the wedding, but I think I'll go now." My brows rose as I did faintly recall all the National Parks building employees getting a standard invitation.

We got so many invites to things that it was hard to go to most of them.

She smiled. "Tomorrow night, seven p.m. at the logging site."

"I'll be there." I watched Christine a few more minutes as she built the white five-layer buttercream-icing cake.

"Watch this." She grabbed some sort of flat tool from her bag.

With one hand, she spun the cake display quickly as the other hand used the tool to go around each layer, stripping away the thick buttercream to make the cake more naked.

"Can you grab one of those sawed-off log parts over there?" she asked as she carefully started to pick the cake up off the stand.

I hurried out of the tent and over to the fairy logs and grabbed one of the pieces of wood.

"Great." Christine looked it over and approved. "Put it on the table."

I laid it on the table, and she quickly removed the five-tiered cake from the stand and placed it on the piece of wood. She stood back and smiled.

"Now, with the greenery Jessica is bringing, it'll look like a fairy cake." She picked up the tool with all the icing on it. "Have a swipe." She took her finger and dug it down into the sugary goodness and stuck her finger in her mouth.

I followed suit.

"Mmmmm." I closed my eyes and let the treat creep down into my soul for a little comfort.

"If you think that's good, just wait until you get a piece of cake. Divine." She winked. "I better get going to get ready. Don't you have to get ready?"

"I guess I do."

It was about that time Jessica pulled up in a refrigerated flower van. A few of her employees hopped out of the van and immediately slid the side doors open, taking out several five-gallon buckets filled with water and fresh flowers.

"I'm going to get out of here." Christine patted me. "I didn't want to mention the thing with Hank, but if it's any comfort, I don't blame you for standing your ground on what you want. Too many people end up settling and being miserable after they realize they compromised their dreams."

Christine didn't even wait for me to comment. She walked off and stopped briefly to talk to Jessica. Both of them looked past me at the cake, and I was sure they were talking about the flowers for the cake, but my paranoia always got the best of me.

CHAPTER NINE

T he buzz of the guests was so loud it filtered through the windows of the Milkery's bed-and-breakfast.

Every few minutes, Abby would peel back the curtain in the suite Mary Elizabeth and Dawn had put the bridal party in, and she'd look out.

"I can't believe how many people are here," she'd say every time.

Every time Abby would say that, everyone loved her.

"Hey, kiddo." Dottie lifted up a layer of the pink taffeta skirt. "I wanted to see how you were doing but figured seeing me in this fairy-looking skirt at my age was entertainment enough that everyone will forget their problems."

"Dottie." She was right. It did make me laugh, not because of her age, but because of the dresses Abby had picked out for all of us to wear. "Never in a million years did I ever figure on us wearing such an outfit."

"You and me both." Dottie's feet were pushed down into a pair of flesh-colored flats, spilling over the edges. "Look at this." She lifted her arms in the air and shook them ever so slightly to let the baggy skin underneath wiggle. "Looks like a pound of Jell-O in there."

"We can all do that." I lifted my arms to show her.

"Not if you did Jazzercise." Queenie proudly made all sorts of arm moves without an ounce of wiggle. "I'm telling you ladies that you could tone up. Look at me and my age."

"Can it, Queenie. It's not 'bout you. It's 'bout Abby." Dottie's glare was harsh.

"What?" Abby turned away from the window. "Did you say my name?"

"Youngon', you need to stop lookin' out that window. It's makin' you so nervous you look like you're 'bout to jump outta your skin." Dottie wasn't making anyone feel any better.

"It's almost time, and I don't see Bobby Ray here yet." Abby let the curtain fall as she turned back around to us. "Y'all sure do clean up nice. But I have to admit the image in my head with y'all in those fairy skirts was much different than in real life."

Betts, Dottie, Queenie, and I started to laugh and look around at one another. We did look pretty ridiculous.

"Are you kidding?" I questioned so she'd feel better. I walked over to her and hugged her, using one hand to open the curtain slightly just to see if, by any chance, Bobby Ray's butt was here.

"Can you imagine what the photos are going to look like with all of those vines dangling down among the twinkle lights next to the fairy garden with our pops of pink and your gorgeous cream dress, not to mention the handsome men who are getting out of the cars now?" I pulled the curtain over.

All the ladies rushed over.

One by one, Bobby Ray and the men piled out of the vehicles.

"My oh my. Look at Hank Sharp. Ain't he just the tomcat's kitten?" Dottie oozed then looked at me. "But don't you worry, May-bell-ine. Good thing you cut your giddyup to his wagon because, honey, you ain't never gonna find Mr. Right hangin' around Mr. Wrong."

The sound of music echoed, saving me from having to have any more conversation about Hank Sharp and how good he looked.

He did look good. There was no doubt about it. And he had on his sunglasses, which was how he looked when I first met him. His mysterious eyes were hidden behind them, then bam! Once he took them off, it was his green eyes that literally put a spell on me.

The wedding went off without a hitch, and I was never as happy in my life not to be standing behind Abby, who was standing in front of Bobby Ray, who had Hank standing behind him, facing me. Well, facing the bride and groom but ultimately me.

I tried not to give him a side-eye glance, but every once in a while, my eye would wander, and a few times, I caught him looking at me. That's when I gave myself a pep talk, missing the cue I needed to take Abby's bouquet when it was time for her and Bobby Ray to say their vows.

There were a few snickers from the guests, but we just kept going, and it ended up being a gorgeous wedding. Now, I was counting down to the time the cake was cut so that I could take my slice to go and head back to the campground so I could grab my notebook and write down anything I had going through my head about Henry and his mixed-up problem with this logging business.

It was time to make my slip-away exit with my piece of cake in hand, plus a piece I'd promised to take Rebecca Fraley at the office, and I weaved my way in and out of the tables, of course having to stop a couple of times when someone would say hello.

I already had plans to go there to see what was going on with the logging situation, and I could easily drop her off the piece of cake. Heck, it might even help me butter her up to let me in on what she knew, if anything.

But my escape didn't go without overhearing murmurs of Henry Bryant's scheme or at least what was being portrayed by Violet Rhinehammer, who by the way didn't show up to the wedding, which made me want to get in touch with her to see exactly what angle she was going to take this.

As much as I hated to call her, she was a good source of information, and in the past, we'd been able to help each other out—me using her for information she could get that I couldn't and her using me to feed her the information for her big story.

"Amazing wedding, Mary Elizabeth." I heard a woman say as I passed by with my back to them. "You went all out for Bobby Ray."

"I had to go all out. This might be the only time I get to throw a wedding," I overheard Mary Elizabeth say. "You never know if Maybelline will ever settle down."

"I heard she let a good one go," one of the women at the table commented, making my eyes roll.

"Yes, honey, he was a good one. Did you see him up there in that tuxedo? He looked so good he could be sopped up with a biscuit." It was unnerving to hear her talk about Hank like that even though she was right.

As soon as I walked out from underneath the tent, I turned back around to see everyone before I slipped out. Immediately, my eyes were drawn to Hank.

He did look so handsome in a tuxedo, and his green eyes stood out so much next to the black.

"Stupid weddings." I pounded my fist into the steering wheel of the old Focus. The rattle of the muffler immediately had me thinking I needed to have Bobby Ray look at it next week before it fell off. Then I realized he was going to be off on his honeymoon, and now that he was married, I was sure he wouldn't be right there when I needed him. He had Abby.

"Stupid wedding."

The rumble of the muffler mixed in with the chirping crickets to create an eerie nighttime rhythmic base musical that bounced off the trees. The lightning bugs danced to the sounds, creating a light show of their own.

I slowed a little when I came upon the curve before the left into the entrance of Happy Trails. Once out of the curve, I pressed down on the gas pedal and sped past the old joint, heading for downtown, straight to the Normal Diner.

Not only was I not in the mood for cake, I had a hankering for pie, a piece of Ty Randal's Kentucky bourbon pie.

Slipping in just before midnight, I knew I wouldn't be turned away.

In fact, I hoped I was the only one in there and Shannon was closing. It would give me time to pick her brain about Henry being there to meet Duke last Tuesday.

The diner was a staple in Normal. Everyone came to eat at the diner. Also, everyone was at the Milkery, partaking in the free food and drink there, so the odds of me having the diner to myself were pretty much in my favor.

The diner was just as cute and Southern as the other downtown shops. It was your standard greasy spoon with homecooked meals and was a diamond in the rough. The L-shaped diner had a row of stools against a counter to the left and a few booths along the right side in front of a wall of windows.

Every chair and booth had sparkly pleather that'd seen better days, but I chalked it up to adding character to the place. It was a hole-in-the-wall that was a treasure to find.

"Hey, Mae," Shannon hollered over the register. "Take any seat."

"Just what I wanted to—" I started to say it was just what I wanted to hear, but when I looked around for my pickings—I loved to sit at the counter—Tucker Pyle was sitting on my stool, and next to him was Al Hemmer.

"Ah oh." Al nudged Tucker when they saw it was me. "You're sitting in Mae's seat."

"Is her name on it?" Tucker popped up to his feet like a smart alec and sat back down, saying, "I don't see her name on it. Did you buy this stool?"

"Funny." I gave him the old thumb gesture. "Scoot."

"I think everyone in this town does exactly what you tell them, don't they?" He waited for me to answer, but I just sat down and stared straight ahead. "Am I right?"

Slowly, I turned my head to the right and looked him right in the eyes. "Did you move down?" I asked.

He grinned.

"There's your answer. But I like to think that I'm a good person, and I love to help people out."

"That is true. Kentucky bourbon double slice for you." Shannon set the regular-sized plate, not pie sized, in front of me with a scoop of vanilla ice cream and a spoon, along with a piping hot cup of coffee. "I saved it back because I was wonderin' if you were going to come in here after the wedding and all." She looked at my pink taffeta tutu. "By the looks of it, I was right."

"Thanks, Shannon." I offered a grateful smile before I acknowledged the point I was trying to get across to Tucker. "Just like this. When Shannon needs me, I'm there. When Al needed me over the summer, I was there. When I needed Al, he was there for me. Now, I need Shannon, and she's here for me. See how things around here work, Tucker?"

"I think I'm beginning to see what Agnes Swift was telling me." He had locked his fingers together and set his folded fists on top of the counter. "She gave me and Al a little talking-to before she left for the big wedding event we weren't invited to."

"Don't you include me in that 'we.' I had to hold down the department. Especially if what Agnes said is true and I might be the next sheriff."

Good luck, buddy, I wanted to tell Al since I knew Hank had it pretty much in the bag if he wanted it.

"Is that right?" I slid my plate over a little to them as an offering of a taste. Both shook their heads.

"Yep. I think I got me a chance, but it was you that she made the comment about that just might be true. Seems like what Tucker said about everyone liking you might play well with us." He looked at Tucker. "Right, Tuck?"

"Er. Tucker."

"Tucker and I do see the value you bring to the table when you put your noodling to helping people, say, in crime cases. And possibly, we could work with you on this thing. Not that I want to step on Sheriff Sharp's toes, but I bet you want to just jab him a little and let me solve this crime." Al talked a pretty big game, and it was tempting.

"Al, I think you'd make a wonderful sheriff." I had to take a drink of coffee to wash that lie down. Al wasn't incompetent, but he needed more experience. "I don't think you need my amateur sleuthing skills to pull anything over Hank's eyes."

"We do need your skills to solve this crime." Tucker drummed his fingers along the counter. "I've never discounted the public and what information is out there on the streets when it comes to clues, so when Agnes mentioned you could be an asset, I knew it to be true."

Al jerked his ear to the side, where his walkie-talkie was strapped on his shoulder, before he jumped up, jerked a dollar bill out of his pocket, and threw it onto the counter.

"Gotta go!" He hollered on his way out.

"Anything to do with Henry?" I questioned.

"Nope. Fire somewhere." He threw two fingers in the air, and out he went.

"Fire. Oh no. Do you think it's a forest fire?" I turned back to Tucker since this was his department.

"Nothing on my end." He'd already pulled out his phone and checked. "Must be a house."

I turned back to my pie.

"How was the wedding? Was it gorgeous?" Shannon walked over and topped off my coffee. "I can make another pot if you think you're going to be staying longer. You can stay while I clean up." She set the empty pot back on the burner and turned around.

"No. This is good. The wedding was great. I've never seen two people so happy. And this pie is amazing."

"I knew it would fill you up and sop up those feelings." She winked and tossed a hip and crossed her arms.

"Say, did you see Henry in here on Tuesday?" I asked.

"I did." She pointed past me toward a booth. "He sat over there. I felt sorry for him. All he wanted was sweet iced tea, and I offered him food. He said he was there to meet someone, but I'm not sure who because they never showed up."

"Can I ask you a question about your cousin Richard?" Tucker or not, I wasn't going to let the opportunity slip by.

"Oh gosh. I heard about Henry. Does Richard have something to do with this? He told his mama, who told my mama that he was on the up-and-up with this new outfit in town." A worried sigh escaped her lips and lay on her face.

"I don't have any information on Richard, but from what I understand, he'd been illegally logging for some time now, and I'm trying to see if Henry knew or not because Hank's got him down in that jail, pegged a criminal." I shook my head, hoping to keep the anger bubbling up inside of me at bay. "What types of behaviors did Richard show?"

"I didn't see it firsthand, but Mama told me that my aunt told her how this man came to the house and offered Richard cash to take down some trees. Once Richard did one job, he said it was easy because the rangers couldn't keep count of the millions of trees here in the forest." The lines between her eyes deepened when she looked at Tucker. "I know you're the new ranger here, but I still think Richard is on the up-and-up. He said he was doing it for the children."

"For the children? What does that mean?"

"Beats me and Mama. We've been trying to snoop around and see if he's done gone and become somebody's baby daddy, but we've come up with nothing." It all rolled so naturally off her tongue. "Anyways, I've got to go clean out the fryers. I'm going to lock the door from the inside, so when y'all leave, just make sure it's closed because the outside can't get in."

CHAPTER TEN

I'd just brought Fifi in from our nightly bedtime walk and made sure the coffee pot was ready for the morning when I heard some rumpus going on outside in the campground.

"Great." I groaned, happy I hadn't taken my outdoor shoes off. "I hate having to reprimand new guests and tell them lights out by eleven, and here it is, midnight."

The rules at the campground weren't any different from any other rules. We did ask for campers to be back at the campground by 9:30 p.m. with the fires extinguished and lights out by 11:00 p.m. It was for not only their safety, but also the safety of the wildlife and environment around us, which made me think about Henry and this entire logging situation again.

"I'll be right back."

Fifi didn't care. She'd already gone out to do her business and was ready for bed herself. She ran back to the bedroom, where I'd meet her shortly.

Or so I thought until I opened the door and all the Laundry Club Ladies were still in their pink tutu bridesmaid dresses, there to pick me up.

"When did you leave the reception?" Betts hung out the driver's side window. "We've been looking all over for you!"

"Grab your notebook! There's been a murder!" Dottie didn't care how long I'd been there, and quite frankly, she made me not care.

"Murder?" I questioned from underneath the camper van's outstretched awning.

"Yep! Duke Weaver is dead!" Dottie did a karate chop to her head. "Ax to the head!"

My mouth snapped shut as the words took shape and hold as my brain wrapped around them.

"Dead?" I asked to make sure the crickets chirping weren't making me believe I'd heard something else.

"*D e a d!*" Dottie spelled it this time, then I heard her ask, "I did spell that right, didn't I?"

As fast as I could, I bolted back into the camper van and slung open the small junk drawer where the Laundry Club Ladies and I kept a spiral notebook of all the snooping we'd been doing over the last few years.

Some of it was just a bit of idle gossip, while some of it really did hold some clues to murders or crimes that happened right here in the Daniel Boone National Park, and right now, this seemed like a crime.

One that could possibly get Henry out of jail.

I would've said goodbye to Fifi, but when I grabbed my real shoes from the bedroom floor, she was already snoring. Yes, she snored louder than any human I'd ever heard.

"Go on!" I hopped into the open back doors of the van and pulled them shut at the same time. "What are we waiting on?"

I sat down in back of Betts's cleaning van between the vacuum cleaner and the mop bucket and changed my shoes.

"Tell me everything. Don't leave out a detail," I told them and opened the notebook since our usual stenographer, Abby Fawn, was off doing what a new married couple did after a big day of stress—sleep.

"When did you leave?" Queenie had gotten a matching pink head-band to put in her hair after Abby picked our fairy dresses. It was plastered to her forehead on one side and drooping down on the other as if she'd been dancing her little legs off.

"I left after they cut the cake, and I might've taken two slices." I licked my lips.

"Okay, so you saw all the dances with Mary Elizabeth and Abby." Queenie was going through the litany of dances Abby had on the agenda.

I rushed them along. "Yes, yes, yes. Get to the part where you found out about the dead body."

"Don't forget to remind us to tell you about Dottie dancing to the Electric Slide." Queenie busted out laughing. When she saw I wasn't smiling or laughing along with them, she said, "Fine."

"After all that bumpin' and grindin' I was doing, my feet were killing me, all sandwiched into them little shoes like sausages. I went inside to the Milkery so I could just slip them off. Then I decided I wanted to go sit on that big front porch of Mary Elizabeth's and have me a smoke while my feet aired out." No matter how serious the story was, Dottie always seemed to make it funny by how she told it. "When I walked through the kitchen, I saw Mary Elizabeth's scanner sitting on the counter. I unplugged it and took it to the front porch. Don't you know there ain't no plugs on that big front porch?"

"That's when Dottie decided to go inside with a lit cigarette, push up the window, and blow the smoke out like she does at home while listening to what was going on around town." Betts caught my eye in the rearview when she was telling me this part of the story. "When Dottie went to ash out the window, an ash fell on Mary Elizabeth's rug."

"How was I to know the darn thing was old and practically dry rotted." By Dottie's reaction, I could only imagine what happened. "That thing caught fire and blew up in flames before I could stomp out a little ash."

"Then the curtains took fire." Queenie shook her head. "That's when Dottie ran back outside yelling"—Queenie cupped her hands over her mouth—"Fire! Fire! Fire!"

"Don't you know the fire department had left their trucks on the logging site, so Hank threw a couple of the fireman at the wedding in his car and drove them out to the site to get the fire truck."

"Luckily, one of the firefighters had gone inside to where Dottie had started the fire, and he was able to use the fountain in the front yard and the water hose on the house to put it out."

"So the entire Milkery bed-and-breakfast didn't go up in flames?" I had to clarify.

"Oh no." Betts maneuvered the big van all over those curvy mountainous roads as I held on. "Just the curtains and the wallpaper on that wall."

"Don't forget the rug," Queenie chimed in.

"It was dry rotted!" Dottie yelled. "That's also when Hank showed up at the site, and a man was lying up against one of the trees with an ax stuck in his head."

"How do we know this?" I asked.

"When the other firefighter was putting out the fire and waiting on the fire truck to get there, the scanner was still blaring through the window, and that's when we heard Hank call in a code thirty." From all the times we'd sat at the Laundry Club drinking coffee, we knew a code thirty meant an officer needed emergency assistance. "Then he yelled out, 'Code one eighty-seven.'"

Murder.

By the time they finished with how Mary Elizabeth had reacted and Tex, our local chiropractor, had been at the wedding and given Mary Elizabeth some sort of natural sleeping medication because she'd taken to bed over the rug, much less the window coverings—forget the burned-up wall, it was the decorations my Southern adoptive mama cared about—we'd gotten to the crime scene. Even before we got up on it, we knew we were headed in the right direction because the blue and red swirling lights filled the nighttime sky.

The scene was already blocked off by the time the Laundry Club Ladies and I had gotten there, along with what appeared to be the rest of the citizens who had a scanner in Normal, which was probably around ninety percent.

"So what's the plan?" Dottie's cigarette bounced up and down from the corner of her lip with each word.

"I suggest we all split up and see what we hear. Remember, nothing is too small. Even if in passing someone says something about logging or land or anything. If you have to use your phone to text it to the group so you can remember it, text it. This is urgent, for Henry's sake." I wanted them to remember anything they could.

"We can meet back here at the top of the hour, which gives us about thirty-five or forty minutes." Betts looked at her watch. "Putting us around eleven."

We all agreed, and I found myself lost in my thoughts as I weaved in and out of the crowd. How on earth did we go from such a great wedding to a tragedy?

The question went away as soon as I noticed the yellow tape holding back the crowd. I stood on the other side of the tape as close as I could get. Hank and a ranger were talking next to a large oak. The trunk circumference was so wide it was hard to see what they were staring at on the other side. With a good guess, I'd venture to say it was the body.

Al Hemmer walked around the tree with the department camera, snapping photos. The flash was so bright I had to look away.

Since the fire truck hadn't made it to the bed-and-breakfast after what happened with Dottie and her smoking, they must've decided it was best to use their lights so the deputies could see in the grass as they searched around for what looked like clues to what had happened to the victim.

"Do we know who died?" I asked the man next to me.

"No." He shook his head. "They've not said a word. Just been shuffling their shoes along the grass and dirt looking for something."

"Thanks." I continued to keep an eye on Hank and see if I could read his lips. He was a great distance away, but the fire truck lights were so bright I was able to see his entire face.

Instead of squinting to see Hank's lips, I turned my attention to the rest of the scene. The tree was marked with a blue X. I wasn't sure if Hank had done that or if it had been done by the logging company.

There were a few long-bed trucks that were used to haul tree trunks out once the trees were cut down, but they were empty and seemed to be parked for the night. The work trailer's windows showed the inside was dark, which told me the logging company hadn't even gotten here yet.

The big cranes and a skidder were pretty close to the tree, so it made me think the tree was next in line to be taken down.

Out of the corner of my eye, Hank had crossed his arms. He and the ranger were looking in the same direction, which made me think the victim was on the opposite side of the tree we could see.

"I can't believe there's another murder in Normal." Violet Rhine-hammer had snuck up on me.

Most times, I could hear her heels clicking as she walked, but not tonight. The grass had kept her secret.

"Did your boyfriend tell you about it?" She snorted. "Oh, that's right —you and Hank are broke up."

I pinched a grin that made my brows rise.

"He does look so good in that tuxedo. I mean, really, if I was at the wedding, I would've made sure my dance card only had his name on each song." She let out a long, deep sigh as she continued to look at him. "But we aren't here for that, are we?"

"We missed you at the wedding," I lied.

"Really?" She lifted her long, thin fingers up to her chest. Her face softened as she flipped her long blond hair behind her shoulder. "I've been working, or I would've been there. With Henry Bryant in jail over this logging situation, I was trying to get to the bottom of exactly where he logged and what effect it was going to have on that particular part of the landscape in our forest."

Her hand dropped, and she took out a tape recorder.

"Do you have any comments on Henry's situation?" She didn't stop at anything to get the scoop for her news broadcast or the *Gazette*.

"Well. I just don't think that Henry knew when someone hired him that he was illegally logging."

"Can you say that one more time?" She clicked the record button on the tape recorder and shoved it in my face.

"That's off the record, Violet."

Hank turned his right shoulder and scanned the crowd. The ranger looked over his left shoulder.

"My oh my, isn't he a delicious piece of pie? New ranger in town?" Violet waved her hand in the air at the two men.

"Sheriff, Ranger, do you have any comments on the body?" She continued to wiggle her hand in the air, bouncing on her toes. "The citizens of Normal have come out to see what is going on, and I'd love to have a statement to put on the news tonight as well as the *Normal Gazette*'s edition in the morning!"

Hank put his hands in his tuxedo pockets and walked over. I tried not to look into his green eyes, but it was hard not to.

"Hank, can I get a statement?" Violet asked.

"We are investigating a crime. We don't have any further information than that." It was a blank statement that he knew would never pacify Violet.

"You mean a dead body is over there? Come on, Hank. Give me something to report. All of Normal is here because they all have scanners, and each one of them know that a code one eighty-seven is murder, victim… whatever it is you want to call it. So just give me something. I'd have to report the appointed sheriff isn't able to keep our town safe, seeing an election is coming up in the fall. I'd hate to see you out of a job." Violet wasn't backing down.

I stood right next to her, happy she was the one asking the questions and not me.

The ranger, whom I'd never seen, walked up next to Hank.

"My name is Violet Rhinehammer. I'm with Channel Two and also the editor in chief of the *Normal Gazette*." She stuck her hand out for the ranger to shake. "You must be the new ranger, Ranger Tucker Pyle."

"Yes, ma'am." He gave a slight nod. His rimmed ranger hat covered his eyes. All I could make out was a strong jawline and chin with a dimple in the center.

"Would you like to give a statement about your territory here in the Daniel Boone National Forest?" She glared at Hank during the first part of her question then slid her eyes over to the ranger before a smile curled up on her lips.

"Well, ma'am." The Southern accent gave him a charm that made the poor feel rich and the old feel young. He took off his hat and held it against his chest.

He had thick blond hair underneath that hat—definitely a Southern gentleman.

"I'm from the Maple Springs district down in Mammoth Cave. I'm excited to be here. I certainly didn't want to meet the good folks of Normal this way, but here we are. We currently don't have any updates for you, but I'm more than happy to invite you to the National Parks office in the morning to grab a statement paper from Rebecca Fraley. I'll be updating the investigation daily and in conjunction with Sheriff Sharp. We are going to let him take the lead on the investigation while I address the public."

"Can you tell us anything about the victim?" Violet didn't let the man get a breath before she shouted out the question.

"Right now, all we know is that a male has succumbed to some injuries that we feel were not done by his own hand. Therefore, we are going to treat this as a crime scene, like I previously indicated. We don't have any further information to give you other than we have deemed this a crime scene." He pushed his hat down back on his head and took a card from his jacket pocket. "Here is my card." He gave it to Violet. "You are more than welcome to come by the National Parks Building and get some updated information in the morning. So why don't y'all get on home and get some sleep so we can do our job and have the latest information waiting for you when you wake up in the morning?"

He offered more of a final suggestion instead of an answer Violet was seeking.

I blurted out another question. "Can you tell us how long the victim has been there? There's a man sitting in Sheriff's Sharp cell that has been accused of illegal logging. If the victim is a murder of a logging crime, do you think the two are related?"

Hank's stare bore a hole right through me, but he turned away when Colonel Holz and Natalie Willowby pushed past the crime scene tape as they both pushed the gurney they'd gotten out of the medical examiner van.

That caught my eye. Normally, Colonel used the funeral home's hearse to transport bodies, but it appeared as if they needed the scientific items stored in the van for much more horrific crimes.

"How did the victim die?" I asked. "Since Colonel Holz has brought the medical examiner van, this must be much more than you're making it out to be."

Hank gave me one last look before he started to walk away, leaving the question for Tucker to answer.

"We do not have any information at this time." Tucker was standing by his comment. "I'm happy to let Rebecca Fraley call you and let you know when we have a statement if you'd like to leave your name and number with one of the deputies. What is the name of your news media?" he asked me.

"For goodness sake. This here is Maybelline West. If you knew anything about the ranger post you've taken, you would know Mae is on the National Parks Committee, and she has a vested interest in our park, just as you do." Violet's demeanor had turned on a dime, and I actually liked her giddyup-and-go spirit.

"It's nice to meet you, Mrs. West." He gave a hard nod. "I look forward to working with the committee during my post."

"Ms." I'd felt the need to correct him. "Mae. You can call me Mae."

"The man Mae was talking about, down in the jail, is her handyman, Henry Bryant. Mae owns the Happy Trails Campground, something else you'd know if you had taken time to tour the town." Violet hammered him.

"No wonder you have a vested interest in this case, Mrs. West."

I corrected him a second time. "Ms., um, Mae. I'm sure Henry didn't have anything to do with the illegal logging, so I'd love to talk to you about that in the morning at the office."

"I am familiar with Mr. Bryant, but I can't comment on how this crime scene has or doesn't have anything to do with Mr. Bryant. I invite you to stop by and see Rebecca at the front desk for any updates in the morning." There he went with that update stuff.

He tucked his thumbs into the top of his waistband.

"Again, this is Mae West, and she's had a huge impact on this town. If I had any advice for you, then I'd suggest you use her as an ally. She's helped Hank on a few cases when even his fancy investigation techniques fell short. Mae is able to snoop out things people wearing those can't." Violet pointed at his ranger badge. "I'm not her best friend or nothing. Probably far from it, but I do know that I love Normal. I love the Daniel Boone National Park, and I sure want to be and feel safe in my community, so if you have any need to call upon Mae here, then I'm sure she'd be more than willing to be of service." Violet's lips slammed shut.

"This is the preliminary stage of the investigation. I am sure, after the coroner's initial report, I will have a few questions, and I'm more than happy to consult Mrs. West on them."

"For once and for all, her name is Mae. Not Missus. Her husband is dead." Violet seemed to have reached her limit with the new ranger.

"It was nice to meet you, Maaeeee." Tucker made sure to drag out my name with a little smirk on his face before he turned to go back to the crime scene.

I popped a hip out, and with my hand on it, I asked Violet, "Since when did you start taking up for me?"

"Since I need information now that you don't have an in with the sheriff. Maybelline. Grant. West." She said my name like each one was its own complete sentence. "We are going to have to work together if we're going to keep this community safe, not to mention getting this new ranger in line with our way of thinking. I'm looking for my next big story. Do you think those cute little hiking photos or even promoting the upcoming

Blossom Festival will get me the coverage I need to be seen? No." She wasn't about to stop for me to even answer her. She didn't want me to answer her—she wanted to be heard. "In fact, every single crime story I report on goes viral. Every single time. And if you think I'm going to let some sort of tension between me and you come between me and my big break, you can forget it. Now, how are we going to get this solved?"

"Let's touch base tomorrow," I suggested since I needed time to go over everything that had happened over the past twenty-four hours with Henry and now this. I'd yet to make sense of what happened at the Milkery bed-and-breakfast, which I was going to have to address at some point.

"Sounds good. I'm gonna go interview some people and see if anyone saw anything or knows anything. It wasn't like he was the nicest man on earth. I will touch base with you tomorrow." Violet walked into the crowd. I overheard her saying, "Hello. Don't forget to watch tonight's news. And I'll have a full write-up in the *Normal Gazette* in the morning with the latest details on the investigation."

"Mae?" Al Hemmer had snuck up on me. "Gosh, I'm sorry." He apologized when I jerked around. "Hank asked me to come get you." He lifted up the crime scene tape just enough for me to ease underneath.

I found myself standing far enough from the tree that I was still unable to see what was on the other side of the massive trunk.

"Hey, how you doing?" I asked Hank. Obviously, I could have come up with a better question.

"Let's cut to the chase." Memories of the first time I'd met Hank as well as the emotions flooded back to me. "Our victim is Duke Weaver. The only reason I'm telling you this is because he has been killed with an ax to the head."

There were rare moments when I was rendered speechless, and this was one of those moments, when Hank decided to tell me, "And the ax has Happy Trails Campground written on it."

CHAPTER ELEVEN

Hank wasn't confiding in me to let me know Henry Bryant definitely wasn't getting out of jail anytime soon—he was letting me know he was sending Al Hemmer over to Judge Executive Gab Hemmer's house to get a warrant to search the campground property.

Quickly, I rushed around and gathered up Dottie, Betts, and Queenie.

"We've got to get to the campground, and I mean fast." I practically shoved each one inside the van. "We don't have time to dillydally." I jerked the cigarette out of Dottie's mouth as she loafed about, trying to smoke it down.

"Maybelline West, you owe me a pack of cigarettes." Dottie was full of piss and vinegar as she watched me stomp out the smoke.

"Think of it as me saving your life." I pointed at the van. "Get in. Al Hemmer is going to be coming to the campground with a warrant. He's on his way to his uncle's house now to get it, and I want to be sure we are there before he is so he doesn't freak out the guests."

"Oh my goodness. If word gets around that the po-lice is there looking around, no telling what will get posted to social media, and then we might go belly-up. And Abby isn't here to save us with her savvy marketing." Dottie was only saying out loud what I was actually thinking.

The silence in the van was deafening on the way back to the campground. The darkness surrounding us left an eerie feeling lingering in the air. The headlights shone only on the pavement ahead, keeping the secrets of the night in the depths of the Daniel Boone National Forest.

"So I was thinkin'." Dottie broke the silence as we headed up to the entrance of the campground. "If a tree does fall in the woods, does it make a sound?"

"Dottie, why on earth are you thinking about that?" Queenie asked.

"Just curious," she whispered. "Ah oh, too late."

Al Hemmer's deputy's car was already parked at the campground office building.

"Betts, you can let us off here." There was no sense in her taking me to my camper when I knew I was only going to walk back up.

"Do you want us to stay?" Betts asked about her and Queenie.

"Nah. There's no reason. Why don't we meet for coffee bright and early at the Laundry Club, and we can talk about it then." It was a good plan since we had no answers to what they might find here.

Al Hemmer must've noticed it was us because he got out of his car and stood next to it, watching me get out.

"Mae, don't be trying to stop me from getting that warrant. Hank said you might do that and I'm to stand my ground." Al Hemmer placed a hand on his utility belt.

"Maybelline, you go on down to let Fifi out, and I'll take care of Al." Dottie was already sore on him. She claimed he was like a kid in a candy shop when his uncle had him put on the sheriff's department. She pretty much told everyone it was underhanded because Al wasn't able to do anything else but ride around the forest all day, looking for an opportunity to take his gun out. In her famous words, she said he was itching to shoot that thing.

"Why on earth would she do somethin' as foolish as that, Al?" Dottie didn't let him speak when he opened his mouth. "Now, you can take your hand off that gun, and we will go inside and get the keys to the toolshed and Henry's camper."

"I don't even have the warrant delivered yet. My uncle is going to do it." Al must've gotten orders from Hank to come here and wait for the warrant so I wouldn't somehow block it.

"I'm not going to stop you from looking." I couldn't hold my tongue. "I'm more than happy to cooperate with the law, especially since Duke Weaver hired Henry to take down those trees because he framed Henry for someone who ended up killing Duke so Duke would stay silent forever."

Al's brows wrinkled together. His eyes narrowed as if he were noodling what I was saying before he opened his mouth then quickly shut it. He shifted his body weight a couple of times and even let out a few huffs. At least thirty seconds went by before he did say something.

"Now, I don't know about all that, but I know I'm to wait here for the warrant while Hank pulls other deputies off the scene to come here to help look for—"

"Look for what, Al?" Dottie snickered. "The ax is in the man's head. That's your evidence. It's not like Henry brought him here to have s'mores or knock back a few cold ones before he practiced ax throwin' out by the logging site."

"Okay. That's enough," I said. The last thing I needed was for Al to call Hank and tell him he was right that we weren't cooperating. "We have nothing to hide. We will wait here for the warrant then hand you the keys or let you in wherever you need to go."

"Thank you, Mae." Al smiled. When he looked at Dottie, the smile faded.

"Can I get you a coffee?" I asked and heard some gravel pinging against tires in the distance, a sure sign someone was driving up.

"That would be mighty nice of you, Mae. It might be a long night. The boys would love it."

"Dottie, do you mind making some coffee in the office, and I'll be in directly." It was a good time to get her out of here since it was the judge pulling up to park.

Dottie harrumphed on her way inside.

Al and Gab said a few words between them as Gab handed Al the warrant out the window. I gave a wave when Gab glanced my way before he drove back off into the night.

It wasn't too long after that a couple of the deputies pulled in, and before long, I'd given them the keys they requested and sent them on their way.

"This just ain't right." Dottie sat at her desk with a zipper makeup bag she used to store her hot-pink sponge curlers. She was keeping her hands busy by taking pieces of her short red hair and twisting them around the sponge curlers before snapping the plastic holders in place. "Do you reckon Henry killed that man?"

"I don't think so, but you never know about people." I told her how I'd tried to put the doubt in Al's head for a reason, to get Al on our side and maybe question anything Hank was doing at the department. "It sure doesn't look good."

I walked over to the window and pulled back the curtain to see nothing but a darting circle of lights created by their flashlights.

"What on earth could they be looking for?" Dottie had half her hair already snapped in the curlers before I got back to my desk.

"I don't know. Maybe a motive." But it was clear Henry didn't really have a motive. What didn't make sense was that he'd done the job. He took down the trees, but why would he have killed the man who hired him? "One thing is for sure."

"Yeah, what's that?" Dottie finished rolling up the last strand of her hair.

"The initial autopsy report will tell us a time of death. If Duke Weaver had been sitting there for a while, then Henry could've possibly done it. But if he was killed today, someone else wanted to keep him quiet."

"I swear, Maybelline, maybe you should run for sheriff." Dottie smiled like a possum.

CHAPTER TWELVE

"If for one second Hank Sharp thinks that ax in that man's head belongs to Henry"—Dottie started fussing while the sheriff's deputies were going through Happy Trails Campground's storage unit, where Henry kept all the equipment—"they are nuts."

We'd been up all night in the office, taking cat naps now and then while Al and the other couple of deputies scoured every single blade of grass and poison ivy leaf to find any sort of clue.

The sound of dragging sacks echoed across the storage room floor, and I was sure they were moving the heavy bags of birdseed we'd stored in there for all of the bird feeders around the campground. It was a good way to make sure the wildlife and unique birds to the Daniel Boone National Forest made appearances. It was a little trick for the birds to make the experience for the campers a little more authentic.

"What was that?" Dottie jumped at the sound of some sort of box crashing to the ground.

"Who knows?" I sighed.

"Henry has that unit spic-and-span clean. If he comes back and sees it's a mess, he'll have a heart attack." Dottie's brows furrowed. "You think he's comin' back. Right, Maybelline?" There was a nervous tone to her and a fear in her eyes.

"I sure hope so. It doesn't help matters that it's taken Al and them all night to look through things. They are being very thorough." It did make me nervous how long they'd been here.

I'd told myself through the course of the night that I'd stay up just a half hour longer. Here I was, seven hours later.

"Hank said the ax had our stamp on it, which Henry does do that so he doesn't get his tools and the campground tools mixed up." I shook my head then said, "Let's go on to the laundromat. I told them we'd be there this morning. It's not doing us any good sitting here wondering when we could keep finding out clues to help him."

There were plenty of people I could go see, but it was too early to do it. Besides, most of them were probably getting ready for church.

"Let me get my curlers out of my hair, and you come pick me up." Both of us got up. Fifi followed suit.

"I'll lock up," I said when Dottie went to grab her keys out of her cigarette case. "Come on, Fifi. Let's go eat."

The campground wasn't as busy this morning. Most of the weekly guests had driven out yesterday, which was when their week lease for the lot was up, unless they'd booked a couple of weeks.

During the busy months, there was a two-week maximum to stay, or we'd have the same people here all spring and summer. Not that it wouldn't be steady income, but it was purely business for me to keep the door rotating so we'd get as many people in here that loved to stay here so they'd book for more time or tell their friends about it.

Though Abby Fawn, um, Abby Bond was amazing at marketing, there wasn't any sort of marketing better than grassroots word of mouth. And there was no better handyman than Henry Bryant.

"I should stay here." I talked to Fifi because I knew she understood my emotions, and right now, all the work that needed to be done looked like it was going to be more than one person could do.

Get the bungalows' special packages delivered before the next guest check-ins. Go through the payments and see who had early check-in. Print all the agreements off so they are ready for the guests. While Betts cleans the campers and the bungalows, grab the flower arrangements from the refrigerator and

take inventory of flowers, donuts, coffee, and cookies for the upcoming hospi-
tality room at the recreation building. All the things I needed to do clicked
through my brain, as did the things Henry did.

Get all the tools from this past week's campfires cleaned and put back on
each side of the bungalow and campers. Refill the firewood for all campsites.
Check canoes. Check paddleboats. Check tiki bar. Check all of the outlets for
hookup. Check the laundry room and machines. Make sure the vending
machines are stocked. Check all the video games. Make sure the volleyballs,
basketballs, and various other balls are filled with air.

The list went on and on.

"We are going to have to put that in the back of our head until I get
back." I unlocked the camper van door and opened it wide for Fifi to
jump up.

Instead of taking a full shower, I took a spit bath, changed clothes,
gave Fifi a scoop of food, and made sure she had fresh water before I
grabbed my keys and notebook and headed to the car to pick up Dottie.

"Do you mind using my phone and texting Beck Greer? I need him
to come help out with getting the campground ready for the new
campers." I handed Dottie my phone.

"You know his mama makes him stay at church all day." Dottie was a
negative Nelly today. It had to be due to the lack of sleep.

I was trying really hard not to go down that road with her.

"Maybe." I shrugged and headed out of the campground toward
downtown. "But it doesn't hurt to try."

The tall trees rose above the curvy mountain road leading to town
as if they were brushing the sky. The sun had risen up them and created
a flickering shadow of leaves and shade as I drove under them.

The morning time gave a nice cool temperature that made it hard to
keep the windows closed, so I cranked down the window and let the
wildflower scents coming off the side of the road float into the car.
Every once in a while, an earthy smell would pass by, reminding me of
the forest we lived in. With each season came life and death. The earthy
smell was decomposing leaves, animal scat, and rotting wood.

The thought of the end of life brought me right back to Henry and the real possibility of him being Hank's number-one suspect. There was a lot that hinged on the coroner's report.

I pulled into an empty space in front of Trails Coffee Shop so I could go in and grab some fresh coffee from Gert Hobson, though I was sure Betts had made coffee. I needed something good and strong, like one of Gert's specialty dark-roast coffee blends.

"Why are we here?" Dottie looked out the window.

"I'm going to get some good hot coffees and maybe a couple of quiche bites for us. We need fuel." I reached into the back seat and grabbed my bag. "Do you want to come in or walk on over to the Laundry Club?"

The Laundry Club was across the center median that divided Main Street into two one-way streets. The two shops were pretty much opposite each other.

"I'll meet you over there. I can walk and smoke." She opened the car door and got out.

Dottie headed across the street, looking like a freight train going through town, while I headed into Trails Coffee Shop.

"I just saw a bunch of wildflowers on the drive here and knew your wall would be so alive today." I loved coming into the coffee house, not only for the awesome coffee, but also for the coolest living wall.

Gert had hired an architect to design the feature so she could display all the unique plants, flowers, and greenery local to the Daniel Boone National Forest for the customers.

"The wildflowers are so amazing this time of the year," Gert called out from behind the counter, which was filled with chrome espresso machines, bean grinders, industrial coffee carafes, and various bottles of flavoring and shakers full of delicious toppings. "Probably when the wall is my favorite."

I couldn't help myself. I walked over and touched and sniffed the flowers, which delighted the eye with all the color pops of purples, blues, yellows, reds, and oranges.

"It's already busy this morning," I noticed.

The mix of café tables, along with long farm tables, was already taken up by customers.

I moved in and around the tables to get to the counter, dodging all the purses that dangled off the backs of chairs and people working on their laptops.

It was the special touches besides her coffee that made Trails Coffee Shop such a unique coffee shop. She'd used so many little added touches from around Kentucky, like the old bourbon-barrel lids she had repurposed into lazy Susans for the center of each table. It was a perfect spot to keep little containers of various condiments that coffee shop customers needed to doctor up their coffees the way they wanted.

"Yeah. And from what I'm hearing, there's been another murder?" she questioned over the sound of the crinkling paper as she was fetching a customer one of the blueberry crumble muffins.

"Unfortunately, Henry had taken a job for the guy to take down a couple of trees. Hank Sharp arrested Henry for illegal logging." I glanced up at the specials written on a chalkboard to see what variety of quiches she was offering today.

"Henry?" She was taken aback as much as I had been. "That doesn't sound like him." She handed the muffin over the counter to the happy customer. "What can I get you?"

"I'll take a box coffee set with a full quiche. Any quiche."

The chime of the door being opened and closed made me look back. Another group of early-morning hikers made their way inside.

One of them pointed toward the side yard after he made eye contact with Gert.

"You're going to have to expand," I teased. "Do you know Duke Weaver?"

"Who?" She put a large cardboard box of coffee on the counter next to the register.

"Duke Weaver. He's the man they found at the logging site." I could tell by the way she was giving me a blank stare that she wasn't able to recall him or the name. "Clearly, you don't. I am asking because I'm trying to get some things together for Ava since she's out of town and can't help Henry until she gets back."

"I'm sorry. I don't know him. Is he local?" she asked.

"I'm not sure. And with Abby out of town, I don't have her contacts to get that information." I took cash out of my purse and laid it on the table. "Do you mind keeping your ears open and let me know if you hear anything?"

"Of course." She tapped on the screen of the register before it popped open.

"Keep the change," I told her and grabbed the coffee box and the bag with the quiche.

Before I headed across the street, I looked down the sidewalk toward the Normal Diner. I squinted when I noticed Tucker was back on the stool—my stool.

"Hey. That's my stool." Jokingly, I nudged him, and down he went.

"I had no idea we were dining in with other businesses' food," Ty Randal yelled through the pass-through window of the kitchen, pointing at my coffee and bag from Trails Coffee Shop.

"I'm just popping in to say hello to our new ranger and warn him not to get too comfortable on my stool." It felt natural to be teasing Tucker.

"You know, they aren't going to turn anything up at the camp-ground," I told him without telling him that I knew he knew about the warrant served as well as Duke's death.

"After we parted ways last night, I got the call that there was a death at the Timberwood Project," he said. "I would offer you a coffee, but it looks like you've got an entire box."

I didn't have time to tell him about the Laundry Club Ladies and who we were though I had a hunch Helen Pyle had probably given him the lowdown on everyone and everything in Normal.

"Mae, do you need another slice of pie?" Shannon sashayed down the back of the counter.

"No. I'm just making a pit stop, but before you go, if Tucker sends you a photo of the man that was killed last night, do you think you could text Richard and ask him if this was the man that paid him to do the illegal logging?"

"Sure." She looked between us. "Here, sugar, give me your phone, and I'll put in my digits. You don't have to worry 'bout sending it to Mae. She's got enough on her plate to worry with being the middle-man." Shannon winked at him.

Geez. Men were slim pickings around these parts, and when a new one came to town, all the women were all over him.

"I'm glad you showed up here this morning. Gives me a chance to tell you in person instead of calling in the morning to let you know that I found a couple different proposals at the office after you left. All of them are different environmental groups but the same logger spear-heading it." Tucker took out his phone and tapped open the photos, showing me the documents.

"Duke Weaver." I thought it was too bad he was dead and couldn't talk himself. "It appears that Mr. Weaver has his name on most all proposals that have funneled through the National Parks, not just here. He's not on the Timberwood Project."

"And his body was found at the project site." I smiled. "Tucker, this could be the clue we've been waiting for."

"So this is the Mae West Agnes Swift seems to think is valuable." He leaned a little back on the stool and folded his arms over his chest as though he was waiting for some sort of enlightenment to come out of his mouth.

"What happened when you found Henry had logged illegally?" I asked.

"I shut down all the logging going on in the area and pulled all the permits. They will be able to start back up Monday."

"You stopped all production?"

He agreed with my question.

"The time it took you to go to each site currently logging, pulling permits and investigating, takes a while. Am I right?"

Again, he agreed.

I continued, "It gave Duke enough time get someone new to log if

Richard was his guy and moved to the other side with, say, Timberwood Project."

"That's a little too tidy for me."

"What's your theory?" I asked.

"I think your handyman, Henry, got caught up into something bad, and timber prices are up. The man took the lumber and left town to get a premium price. I think he went back to the Timberwood Project. He was checking things out. Was going to steal some timbers on the ground."

"And Henry took the ax and killed him?" I shook my head. "Doesn't make sense."

"I'm not saying any of this makes sense, but we don't have enough clues to say one way or the other."

"I tell you what, I'm pretty confident Henry didn't do it. If I'm wrong, I will personally take you on a few trails as the National Park Committee member and show you the very popular ones that most tourists take and that most tourists need help on. If you're wrong." I tapped my temple because there wasn't much I needed from him.

"If I'm wrong, I'll bake you a Kentucky bourbon Pie." He drove a hard bargain.

"Deal." We shook on it before I once again headed over to the laundromat, where I was sure they were wondering what was taking me so long.

The median wasn't as crowded like it will be this afternoon. The flags we'd approved at the National Park Committee for the upcoming Blossom Festival had already been hung up on all of the lantern posts that ran alongside the sidewalk and dotted throughout the park.

The Blossom Festival was also a new event added to the already packed festival schedule. The board felt like we needed something in the summer besides the reason over ninety percent of people come here, and that turned into the Blossom Festival.

Anyway, I couldn't help but notice the flags looked nicer than I thought when the graphic artist the committee hired had given us the mock-up with its large green leaves and white-blossomed trees.

That was another reason to get the murder solved and in the back of everyone's minds. The festival was a few weeks away, and if anyone heard about a murder happening right here, they'd probably take a hard pass on visiting.

"We were just about to get started." Betts met me at the door and took the box of coffee from me. "I don't have a lot of time since I'm teaching Sunday school this morning, so let's get this show on the road."

"Sounds good to me," I agreed and followed her past the row of washing machines as they whirled and slurped. On the other side of the room, loose coins pinged inside of the dryer with each tumble. Betts kept a jar full of loose change from machines and stuck it next to the vending area for people to use and take what they needed.

She was such a good person.

"Any news from Beck?" Dottie asked when I sat down.

"Not yet." I pulled my phone out again to look at it in case I'd missed hearing it chirp when I was at Trails Coffee Shop but found nothing. I put it back in my purse and took out the notebook, but before we could even get situated, the bell over the door dinged.

We turned around, thinking it was going to be one of the campers or hikers in the area to do some laundry, but it wasn't. It was Violet Rhinehammer with a stack of the *Normal Gazette* in her arms.

"Good morning, ladies." She greeted us and set her handbag on one of the couches to the right of the door in the television area. "I do love me a good jigsaw puzzle." She gestured at the one half completed on the table in the game section of the laundromat.

"She's swinging her hips like the church bell on Easter," Dottie muttered, making Queenie snort.

"What was that, Dottie?" Violet asked and politely handed each one of us a newspaper. "Did you say something about church? Because I am on my way there. That's when I noticed all of y'all in here, and I said, now Violet, you and Mae had an agreement. Surely, she and the ladies aren't in there discussing all the goings-on with Duke's murder and Henry's current situation without calling you because she promised."

She directed her third-person narrative toward me as she sat down on the edge of one of the chairs. She crossed her ankles.

"Am I right, Mae?" she asked, her brows arched high upon her forehead.

"You made an agreement with the devil?" Dottie asked with Betts and Queenie eyeballing me. "Just in case you were unclear who that might be, it's Violet."

"Now, Dottie, if it weren't on Sunday and I was about to go to church, I just might take offense to that, but seeing how you yourself just set Mary Elizabeth's house on fire, I'd stop talking." Violet glared at Dottie.

"I didn't catch anything deliberately on fire. Besides, you don't know. You weren't even there." Dottie's lips twisted.

"Oh dear. The wedding. The photos are gorgeous. They made it into the society page, which has the best photo of Hank Sharp smiling." She threw a look my way. "But the even funnier one is of Dottie trying to throw what little iced tea she had in her glass at the burning curtains." She giggled and threw her hands at us. "But you can read that on your own time. Since we are here to solve a murder."

"What?" I asked the Laundry Club Ladies and shrugged when they were giving me all sorts of eye vibes. "We are here for the greater cause. Get Henry off the hook. Now that Abby is off on her honeymoon, we don't have those resources, but we do have Violet, and she does have a lot of resources, one of which I thought of something you need to find out." I opened the notebook. "Where does Duke Weaver live, and does he have a real job?"

"Great minds, and I already looked into that because I just knew you'd want to know. I keep all my records on my phone." Her long nails clicked on the glass screen of her cell phone. "I just sent you his home address."

As soon as she said that, my phone chirped from the bottom of my purse.

"That's me." She winked. "And we need to note that Mr. Weaver wasn't the nicest guy in town. I had an interview with him years ago when he was on some sort of logging board back in the day. He was rude and nasty."

"This situation is not to be taken lightly. We the Laundry Club Ladies are very serious about things that we look into, and we can't let anything leak this time because Henry Bryant is our dear friend, and he did not do this. Here is what I do know." I got up and started to pace while the Laundry Club Ladies and Violet listened as Betts gave them cups of coffee and slices of quiche.

"Duke Weaver is the name of our victim. He was killed with an ax from the campground. At least, that's what we were told, and when Dottie and I left to come here, the deputies were still at the camp-ground, scouring every single inch," I said without opening the notebook.

"We don't have much time. We've already wasted a lot of it while I've been here." Violet tapped the top of her watch with her fingernail. "And I've only gotten two thousand steps in so far."

"If you came to Jazzercise, you would get around five thousand in a class." Queenie gave a one-shoulder shrug and brought her coffee up to her mouth.

"Violet is right. I've got to get to church. Are you ladies going to come this morning?" Betts sure did know how to silence us. "I think Mary Elizabeth could use some moral support this morning."

"I've even got some lipstick you can put on." Violet smiled, knowing Mary Elizabeth would forgive the outfit I had on, but not bare lips.

"Of course I'll go support Mary Elizabeth."

"She's going to be so happy." Betts looked happier than how I antici-pated Mary Elizabeth would be.

"Okay. Back to this." I wagged the notebook up in the air. "This is what we know."

I opened the notebook and started to read what I had written last night after we got back from the crime scene and while I waited up all night in the office.

I repeated, "The victim is Duke Weaver. The weapon is an ax that can be traced back to Happy Trails Campground. There will be a preliminary report this morning, and I can go pick that up after church at the National Parks Office. Tucker said Rebecca would be there with the report. We also know Duke Weaver has been on several proposals to log, not just in the Daniel Boone National Park, but all different parks. And each time, they've been turned down. He's not part of the Timberwood Project."

Everyone nodded their heads like they were with me.

"Do you think someone from the Timberwood Project killed him?"

"Possibly. Good chance. I will also pull the proposal that the Environmental Group of Animal Habitat has on file for this job." I proceeded to tell them how permits were written and whose names were on them and how they were filed. That was a good first step to see who had access to that area.

"If Abby was here, I'm sure she'd be able to tell us more about him, with all of her contacts, but we are just going to have to make do." Queenie sat back with a frown. "Good time for Abby and Ava to be gone."

"Don't count me out." Violet smiled, holding her phone out for us to see. "I've got my own list of contacts, and I already sent you his address."

"After I go to the office, I can make a trip to his house if it's not too far," I said.

"Too far" was the operative phrase. With the campground in disarray from the last set of guests leaving and a new crop of them driving in today for the week, and with one man short, Henry, there was no way I could leave Dottie alone.

"He's not too far away. I'll go with you since two sets of eyes and snooping noses are better than one." Violet popped up. "I'll see you ladies at church." She'd already walked up to the couches. "I'll meet you in the vestibule," she told me directly before she picked up her purse and dropped her phone inside.

"You go on with her after church. I'll make sure I get a ride with Beck and his mama." Dottie snapped open her cigarette case to retrieve another smoke.

"Did you get a text from them?" I asked and looked at my phone.

"Nope, but I'll make sure he can come help because you've got to figure out who killed Duke Weaver and who framed Henry for all of it because you and I both know the crapper is always clogged in the men's bathroom at the campground." With the cigarette stuck between her pointer and middle finger, she pointed at herself. "Dottie doesn't unclog the crapper. You get what I'm sayin', May-bell-ine?"

CHAPTER THIRTEEN

If there was ever a time to skip church, it was today. When I got there, Mary Elizabeth wasn't sitting in the front pew. She never showed up. But my luck changed right after we were dismissed.

It was then that I noticed Hank talking to Colonel Holz in the vestibule, where I was to meet Violet. Of course I couldn't just go and interrupt, so like a good Southern woman, I decided to take the side hallway and hang next to the litany of flowers Jessica Niles donated to the church service for her weekly tithe portion, in hopes to hear a smidgen of something.

I positioned myself behind a couple of what looked like tall potted palms that stood as tall as me on either side of a display of various flowering plants in different-sized indoor planters. Luckily, the meditation fountain wasn't on, so I could faintly hear Hank and Colonel outside of the usual "good morning and good to see you" chatter.

"You mean as in two hours before we found him?" Hank asked Colonel.

"All I can tell you is my preliminary findings—he was struck from behind on the back of the head once, and it appeared he turned around, and that's when the last swing got his neck, which ended up slicing the artery right here."

Now, I had no idea what "right here" was because I was relying on my ears to hear and not my eyes to see through the plants.

"There are some marks on his hands where it looked like he tried to shield himself from whoever was swinging the ax." Colonel Holz reminded me the ax was from Happy Trails.

If Henry had been in jail, who took the ax from the campground? And that meant that Henry didn't kill Duke Weaver and the possibility of him having been set up was much greater now.

"Mae, are you eavesdropping?" Violet Rhinehammer had snuck up behind me, nearly causing me to jump out of my skin. She threw a hand over my mouth. "Shhh," she whispered before moving her hand and leaning around me to get a glimpse at what I was hearing.

"I already sent the report to the department, but I'm telling you by the way Duke was dressed I think he was meeting someone there." Colonel was great at making such detailed observations. "He had on house slippers. If he was going to go to the site to actually work, he would've had on a pair of steel-toed boots and a hard hat."

Violet poked me on a shoulder. I looked at her. I couldn't help but notice she had her long hair pinned up in a small bun on the back of her head, nothing like I'd ever seen before.

She pointed for us to go back down the hall the opposite way of the vestibule.

Slowly, we emerged from behind the flowers and hurried down the hall, offering smiling nods to the church members we passed. We took the stairs to the basement, which led us around to the exit that was located on the side of the building and next to the parking lot.

"We can take my car." She had her key fob out, already clicking it a million times to make sure the doors were unlocked so we could quickly get in and make a getaway before Hank or Colonel saw us together.

"Did you hear that?" I asked her. "Henry couldn't've killed Duke."

"I know. That's great. But Duke's dead, and he can't tell us if he hired Henry or why he hired Henry."

"Henry already said Duke hired him. I'm hoping we can get something from his house, maybe a note or something. I even thought about breaking into the construction trailer I noticed on site to see if he had anything to do with that." I gnawed on my cheek. "One problem—I think we need to head to the office to get the logging proposal we approved. If Duke's name is on that, then maybe someone from the logging company or the environmental group killed him."

"Did Henry say if anyone was with Duke when he hired him?" she asked and headed the opposite way of the campground, toward the National Parks Office.

"He said it was just Duke." Now, I had some leverage to get Henry out of jail now that he wasn't a suspect on murder charges.

While Violet drove, I texted Dottie to make sure she got Beck, then I texted Ava to let her know Henry wasn't a suspect in the murder of Duke Weaver, asking her to work her magic so I could get Henry out of jail today even though he was still facing illegal logging charges.

"Mary Elizabeth." My words caught in my throat when I heard her answer the phone in a low and sad voice. "I'm so sorry about the bed-and-breakfast. Is there anything I can do?"

"I heard you came to church today. Betts and the Bible Thumpers brought me over some flowers from the altar and said they missed me. Wasn't that the kindest gesture ever?"

"I'm sorry I didn't make it over yet. Since Henry is in jail, Dottie and I've got a lot to do before the guests arrive this afternoon, and you know how busy that gets." I was trying to make myself feel better about not going to go see her. "I thought I'd see you at church. Do you think I can stop by sometime tonight or tomorrow? We can make a plan to get that room fixed up in no time."

"Alvin Deters already said he'd donate whatever material I needed. Wasn't that nice of him?" I could hear the shock she was still in by the tone of her voice.

I could clearly tell I was going to have to make the decision of when to see her.

"Does Dawn have everything taken care of so you can rest?" I asked, and she assured me Dawn was on top of everything, which I didn't doubt. "Why don't I bring some supper by tomorrow night?"

"That's good, honey." She agreed, but it sounded like whatever Tex had given her was making Mary Elizabeth agreeable to everything, which was entirely unusual.

We said our goodbyes just as Violet was pulling up to the old brown building.

It wasn't anything spectacular and grand. Not many dwellings were in the forest, due to the mold, rain, and humidity. It was best to keep good solid material on the outside of buildings and homes so they were easily cleaned without a lot of maintenance.

"Let's go." Violet turned off the car, and we got out.

CHAPTER FOURTEEN

"Hey there, Mae!" Rebecca Fraley was sitting at the first desk when we went into the rangers' station when I walked in the door. By myself.

Violet had gotten a phone call she'd insisted on taking, so I left her in the car while I went on inside.

Rebecca's brown football-helmet hair was never out of place. She had on a short-sleeved blue-striped cotton shirt. "How was the wedding? I bet Bobby Ray and Abby are beaming. Mr. and Mrs. Bobby Ray Bond. Abby Bond." She looked down at her wedding ring. The pearlized nail polish, which was the only nail polish she ever wore, gleamed to a high shine.

"It was great. I'm sorry you weren't able to make it." I leaned on the counter and nonchalantly glanced around at the other desks to see if Tucker was around.

"I really, really wanted to go, but like I told you when I dropped off those brochures, someone had to work." She pointed to herself. "Low man on the chain. Plus, I was glad I was here with everything going on." She shook her head and sat back in the chair. She gestured for me to sit down. "I'm 'bout to retire, and then I'll have all the free time in the world."

She continued, "I mean, Henry Bryant of all people." Her eyes grew bigger with each word that fell out of her mouth. "I mean, that is a major crime to be logging land around here. You know that."

"I do." At least she was talking about it, and it occurred to me that she could be a good source of information. "I know I can't believe it myself. Which you know Henry as much if not better than me. That's why I'm here. I met Tucker the other day. He mentioned he was the one who found the trees had been logged and on the case for our committee. Is he in yet?"

She looked over her shoulder as she leaned up on her forearms.

She whispered, "He is. He's so busy, you know, with the first case and all. He's really trying to do a thorough job, and he asked not to see anyone." She gnawed on her lip. "He even mentioned you by name." She frowned. "I was hoping you wouldn't come in because I sure didn't want to hurt your feelings."

"You didn't hurt my feelings. He's heard I'm pretty darn good at solving such mysteries, and well, like you said, it's his first crime at his new post." It was time I told her. "I've talked with him a couple of times about the case, and he did mention you were going to have the latest on it for us to pick up."

"Well, you know this is his new territory." Rebecca was telling me, in her own way, not to be hurt. She reached over and handed me a piece of paper that had Official Statement typed in the center of the page.

"Yeah, no, I get it. And you know, I just want to make sure that he knows that since I'm on the National Park Committee and that Henry is an employee of mine, that I wasn't going to mix the two. Especially since the park committee did pass the Timberwood Project, which included logging all those trees right around the area Henry had cut down the trees. In no way, shape, or form did I have anything to do with illegal logging."

It wasn't that I was trying to act as though I'd not already covered all of this with Tucker—I really wanted to see what she knew, and instead of just flat-out asking her, I tried this technique.

"I don't think he thinks that. He had asked me a few questions about you and your past with the campground and all." She continued to yammer on and on like she was trying to make good with me.

This was what tuned me in to the fact Rebecca knew more than she was telling me. She was uncomfortable with me standing there and was filling the silent air between us. I also knew if I stood there long enough, I'd get so much information from her trying not to give me information.

"Tucker said something that maybe Henry was saving up the money because winter was going to be here before we knew it and he's talked to his cousin, Helen. Did you know Helen Pyle is Tucker's cousin?"

I nodded, thinking Tucker hadn't said that to me. Come to think of it, he'd never told me what his theory was.

"Of course you did. I've said too much." She gestured. I stood there and continued to stay silent until she couldn't stand it anymore. "Anyways, Helen told him that Ann Dougherty told her how you have a winter account down at the bank and you put money in there or Henry puts money in there for you and himself to help get by in winter."

She shrugged.

"It's that way for everyone in the Daniel Boone National Forest. You know, slow winter months." Rebecca looked down at her desk and shuffled through her papers.

"Winters can be brutal, but I'm sure Tucker already knows that with family here and all." I made the observation.

"I told him how good you've done for yourself, especially all the reservations for Happy Trails Campground even though you spend a lot of your time helping Hank and finding all those dead bodies, bringing all them killers to justice."

"Oh, Rebecca." I groaned after I'd heard enough. I'd never mentioned Hank to him and hadn't planned on it. "Why on earth did you have to tell him all that?"

"I just wanted Tucker to see what a good and fine, upstanding citizen you are and how the gossip down at the Cute-icles is just hearsay and not gospel. Heck, the prayer line at the Normal Baptist Church is just a nonguilty way of gossip too."

That's when I knew it was all over town, how the news of Tucker's feelings about me was already circulating around town.

"Oh now, Mae, you know it doesn't matter. It doesn't matter what he says. It doesn't matter what people think." Rebecca reached over her desk and patted my hand.

"It totally matters what people think. I have spent the better part of two years trying to get over what people think."

"He mentioned that you were bullheaded and that you didn't take no for an answer and that you can stick your nose into everything, but not that…" She hesitated when she saw me jerk back. "That's not a bad thing because everything has turned out so good. I started to tell him how fancy you are and how fast you turned the campground around with your determination."

There were some rumblings in one of the rooms behind her.

She started talking fast.

"I told him you were one big ball of fire and he could use your help because everyone in town loves you. I also told him that you'd probably go to the ends of the earth to help Henry because he's been so loyal to you. That's when they told me they had Henry on camera just sawing away at them trees. He just ain't gonna get out of that one. Now that guy is dead. Henry put that money in the bank. It just doesn't look good."

"I'm going to have to stick my nose in it. Today, I'm going to see what Lloyd Hornbuckle and Judge Hemmer know."

Lloyd was the board president, along with Judge Hemmer as a committee member.

"Lloyd Hornbuckle and Judge Hemmer—both told Tucker you were quite qualified to be on the board and that they did take into consideration the kayak incident and the bow-and-arrow incident at the campground." Her voice trailed off as she reminded me of a few situations I'd really tried hard to erase from my mind and the minds of any guests that were staying at Happy Trails Campground at the times of these incidents. "I think I better just shut up."

I laughed.

"It's okay. I guess all of those things made me good at snooping around." I really wasn't hurt by all the information Rebecca had told Tucker. I guessed I just wasn't prepared for it. I liked to be prepared.

"The more I talked to him about you, the faster he wrote."

"He was writing down what you were saying about me?" I found that odd.

"Ahem." Rebecca continued, "I'm so excited for Bobby Ray. I know Abby is over the moon." Rebecca's dramatic gestures made me look around to see who she was acting for.

"Hello again." Tucker looked me up and down with an arrogant appraising eye.

"Hi." I smiled.

"Mae's brother got married to Abby Fawn this weekend. Abby is the librarian." Rebecca's nervous energy was revibrating around us.

"That's nice. I'm going to be going out for a minute." He nodded. "Mae, would you like me to walk you to your car?"

I wondered what on earth could be taking Violet that long.

"Yeah, that would be great." My brows rose as I looked at the file in his hand. "Anyways. It was good seeing you again, and I will talk to you later, Rebecca."

"Yeah, you too. By the way, did you get your hair straightened at Cute-icles for the newspaper article?" Rebecca asked.

"What newspaper article?" I pushed my unruly curly hair back, knowing there was no way I could get my hair straightened in this humidity. Nor had I had it straightened in a while.

"The *Normal Gazette* article by Violet Rhinehammer." Her mouth popped open. "I'm guessing the picture was old and you've not seen the newspaper today."

"Unfortunately, I haven't seen that yet, but I am sure that Violet Rhinehammer did me justice." I wouldn't be so sure about that.

"I also sure hated to hear about you and Hank."

"Yeah." I tapped her desk and stood up. "Good seeing ya."

I couldn't get out of there quick enough. I could feel her judging eyes on me when Tucker and I walked out of the office building.

"Here's copies of the proposals I was telling you about. I've also included the Timberwood Project so you could get all of the names and see what your contacts can find out."

"Contacts?" I laughed and took the file.

"Agnes said you had contacts. I need help. You have contacts." He threw his hands up. "Good?"

"Perfect." I slipped the file up under one armpit and tried not to bust out laughing at Violet Rhinehammer being my contact.

CHAPTER FIFTEEN

"Well, I guess I should've looked at the photos in the newspaper this morning." I slammed the car door when I got back in. Violet was taking notes on a piece of paper.

"I put in there a good photo of you with your hair straight. You should thank me." She leaned back in the driver's seat and looked me up and down.

"Who was on the call?" I asked.

"I got a witness who said Duke Weaver had an argument with someone by the name of Andrea Burt."

"I think we might have our suspect." I wiggled in the air the file Tucker had given me. "Andrea is the foreman—forewoman—in charge of the Timberwood Project. Tonight is the ribbon-cutting ceremony."

"I'm going to it," Violet said.

"I am too. And now that you have someone who said they saw them arguing, it shows the victim knew her and he was found dead on her project site." This was all starting to fit together. "Did your witness say they'd come forward to tell the sheriff what they heard?"

"Not yet. If I can prove Andrea Burt had something to do with the murder, he said he'd come forward." If there was a good quality about Violet that I could appreciate, it would be her ability to keep her mouth shut and honor her word when it came to informants off the record and all things dealing with secrets—if she was told to keep a secret.

That was a very rare trait around here. When I did call the Laundry Club Ladies out on it one time, they told me it wasn't gossip but a form of praying. *Mmhhmm.* I didn't buy that at all because their "praying" was always followed up by a "bless her heart."

"I guess we need to focus on how we are going to do that." Violet's observation lingered in the air. "And I think we need to go over to Duke's house." She fingered at my phone. "Put the address in your maps. I kinda know where it is, but I think there's been a lot of construction on the roads to help with all the flooding over the spring."

Flooding was something very common in the Daniel Boone National Forest. When the spring rains fell, the natural water springs, creeks, lakes, ponds, and any body of water within the forest would rise. They would spill over the banks and onto the road, creating many different types of landslides, which caused the asphalt on the roads to chip and be swept away.

Just like Violet had said, the early summer months were when the park committee was busiest with the Kentucky Transportation Department, getting the roads fixed as quickly as possible and with as few road closures as possible. Luckily, there were more ways than one to skin a cat, pardon the expression, but it meant around here that there was more than one road that took us where we needed to go. That could be a long, winding gravel road, but there was always another way.

"Looks all clear." I used my fingers to enlarge the map from where we were to Duke's address. "Nothing looks closed." I set the phone on the dash so Violet could hear the directions while I told her what had happened while I was in the office when she was outside on the phone with her informant.

"We know Duke has been on several proposals, but none of them have passed, which leads me to believe he definitely was doing something to undermine the Timberwood Project." I had in my lap the files Tucker had given me, and I quickly scanned them. "If I had a hunch, Duke must've thought if he cut down some trees near the actual project and the rangers would go out to check, they'd see the trees not in the proposal were taken down."

"Which is illegal and would shut down the project, possibly opening it up to another logging company." Violet finished my theory.

"Yes. He asked around and figured he'd use Henry, but I'm not sure if Duke intended for Henry to get caught. If I had to make another educated guess, I'd figure Duke didn't know the rangers in our district actually put up hunting cameras to make sure the work is getting correctly complete and that's how they found Henry on there."

"That's good," Violet agreed.

"And I think tonight at the ribbon-cutting event, I'm more than happy to snoop around to see what we can find out. Maybe even question Andrea Burt to see what she knows." All of this suddenly felt very personal.

While I wondered and tried to remember the layout of the logging site from when we were at the scene of the crime, nothing but the work trailer, the skid trucks, and flatbeds that hauled out the timber stood out to me.

I didn't say it out loud, but one possibility was to get into the trailer tonight when no one was watching so I could try to find anything that connected Andrea and Duke to one another.

With another quick search of the papers Tucker had given me and all the names listed for each job site, I didn't see anything on there with Duke's and Andrea's names. That didn't mean anything. I'd been on the committee long enough to know there were change orders and workers being filed and approved all the time.

Unfortunately, that type of search took a long time, and I wasn't sure if Henry had that time.

"Here we are." Violet pulled up to a chalet with a gorgeous view from the front of the house. "This is what I love so much about the forest. All of these neat houses that you'd never know were here are tucked in perfectly." She shut the engine off and twisted around to talk to me. "Have you ever wondered how these plots of land got into people's hands? Honestly, if you think about it, the forest truly isn't that old."

We were proud of our 2.1 million acres of land the National Park Services decided to reserve in 1937, which honestly wasn't too terribly long ago. Of course, there was much more history dating back to the 1770s, but the forest didn't get proclamation boundaries until 1937.

"And this piece of land is probably passed down generationally." I'd heard over and over how lucky I was that I owned the campground land.

Granted, it had been through a hand of poker my ex-now-dead husband won back in college, but it was still how I'd gotten it.

Violet made a great observation. "There's not crime tape up. Strange."

"I would assume since Hank had cleared the crime scene and the logging company is going forward with the ribbon cutting, that they are finished here." I looked at the chalet from the car.

"Then I guess it's okay to snoop." Violet reached into the back seat and grabbed her camera, her real camera. "You never know when you need some evidence."

She pulled the strap over her head and let the camera dangle, resting on her chest. Both of us got out of the car and looked around as we made our way up to the front door.

"He's got one of the camera doorbells." She pointed at the attached white box with the little blue light. "And it works. Which means that if we can get inside, we can see if the settings are set to record and maybe look back a few days, even a week, to see if there were any visitors."

"Great. It also means that we are on here now." I hesitated to reach for the doorknob to see if it was, by chance, unlocked.

"Nah. I have one. I can erase us." She winked.

"Who knew you were so sneaky? I just thought you liked to ask questions to get your answers." I was pretty impressed with Violet Rhinehammer, while I let her do all the dirty work and could with a clear conscience say I didn't have anything to do with clearing a video camera just in case I was asked.

Violet grabbed the door handle, giving it a good jiggle. It was locked. She gestured for me to follow her. We walked along the sides of the house. Every window or door we came to, she tried to open it by the handle or shimmy it up.

On the back of the house was a French door that'd seen better days. Each door had a long piece of glass from the top to the bottom.

"No dead bolt." She grinned and reached up to her hair, where she plucked one of those bobby pins out of her bun. "I'm always prepared."

"I was wondering why you had your hair up." However, this probably wasn't the time to talk about her hairstyle choice.

"I'm always prepared for anything. I knew we were going to come here today, so I thought, hmmm"—she scratched her chin—"how are we going to get into the house? I'm pretty good with a bobby pin."

I took a step back and watched Violet. I started to adore her even more.

She pulled the bobby pin into an L shape. She took a hold of the door handle with one hand and used the other hand to manipulate the door lock with the bobby pin.

"*Voila.*" The door handle turned, and she cracked the door open. "Another thing I learned." She barely opened the door and clicked her tongue a couple of times. "You have to check to see if any animals are in the house. Or at least loose."

"Good thinking." I wouldn't have thought of that and just would've walked right on in.

"I think the coast is clear." We had waited a minute to see if anything or anyone was going to come running at us.

The house was typical chalet native to the area. The bottom floor was where the bedrooms were located, and nothing was fancy about the place. The steps led us up to the top floor, where there was a kitchen and family room with an office off to the side.

"Now to find that Ring camera video unit." She opened a few doors until she found the laundry room. "For some reason, a lot of them are installed in the laundry room. Maybe because of the electrical supply in the wall or something."

She shrugged and started to poke at a machine with a small video screen. I stood behind her and watched over her shoulder, trying to keep every little detail she was doing in my mind just in case I needed to do this one day. Not that I was planning on it, but you never knew just when you did need a skill. This was a skill.

"Violet." She clapped her hands as she congratulated herself. "It looks like he keeps a month's worth of data before it starts to record over itself."

"Which means we might get to see—" I was going to say we might get to see some coming and going, but she already had it rolled back to when someone had come to his door.

"You must be Henry Bryant, the local handyman everyone has recommended." Hearing Duke's voice on the doorbell video camera surprised me. It made me sad, but it also showed Henry had been here. "Come on in and let's talk about some details of the job."

"Did you see that?" Violet jumped around.

"Henry." My heart hurt.

"No. Not the obvious. Did you see how Duke had Henry come in, and then he looked around as though he wanted to make sure no one saw them. Up here? Strange." She rolled back the footage. "See?"

As sure as we were standing there, she was right.

"I wonder who he was looking for. It's odd that, all the way up here, he'd think someone just might be watching him as if he were hiding something already," I noted.

"Oh yeah. He's definitely hiding something, and that something is the logging he hired Henry to do. Unfortunately, the only thing we can hear is what happens at the door. You'll have to go back to Henry and tell him you saw him on camera at Duke's. We need the full conversation. Here." She took the camera from around her neck. "Click the time stamp, and I also want you to flip the switch to video so we can have it on film."

"Why on earth had I not thought of that?" I suddenly felt my sleuthing skills needed a little dusting off.

I got the camera positioned and did exactly what she said to do. We had to review the footage a couple of times, then I played back what we had so we knew we'd gotten it.

She tapped the video tape forward.

"Get this." I pulled up the camera as she let the video roll when Henry was walking out.

"No problem. I've got all the equipment to get them down. They don't seem to be too big, so I figure it's a one-man job." Henry was talking.

"Great doing business with you, Henry. I'll meet you at the diner on Tuesday with your money." Duke had made the arrangement, which I was glad to hear because Henry had already told me this.

"Did you get it?" Violet had stopped the video when Henry walked off.

I nodded.

"Okay, let's see if anyone was there." Violet put the video on two times the speed.

The sun would pop up and then fade, signaling it was morning to night. Not much was going on.

"He seems to be a recluse." I couldn't wait until she got to Tuesday so I could see if he did leave the house to go see Henry or not. "Did you just pass Tuesday?"

"Mm-hmm. Interesting, right?" She looked over her shoulder at me with a raised brow.

"Do you think he just set Henry up to do the dirty work and decided to lay low?" I threw out the theory again.

"Oh look." She hit the back button. "Get this." She was talking about the camera.

"Ready." I steadied the camera up to the doorbell screen and watched someone approaching the door on the camera's small video screen as Duke opened the door.

"Do you see that grin on his face?" Violet noted and made sure her commentary was on the video we were recording. "It's a woman, though we can't see her face from the baseball hat she's wearing. But I'm thinking it's a woman because of the purse on her shoulder."

"Come on in. I was so glad to get your call." Duke invited her in and closed the door without her saying a word.

It was about an hour and a half before the woman left. She didn't leave out the front door. She left out the back.

We forwarded the tape several days.

"There!" Violet jumped for joy. "What's the time?"

"Saturday. Yesterday at five p.m." I'd never been so happy to see him leave, alive. "This shows Henry didn't kill him. He might've logged illegally for him without realizing he'd done it, but he's no killer."

"Which means that Duke left here to go to the logging site because the coroner put his death a few hours before they found him. Which means that whoever killed him wasn't at the wedding, which everyone was at the wedding."

A tear fell from my cheek.

"Are you okay?" Violet looked at me.

I nodded but couldn't say a word.

"Mae, you really care for these people."

"These people?" I laughed. "You have no idea."

CHAPTER SIXTEEN

After a little bit more snooping and turning up nothing else, Violet and I decided to go straight to the sheriff's department. There was no time like the present to get Henry out of jail.

Even though there'd been a murder, since it was Sunday, the building was sparse with deputies.

"Hank, you've got to see it," I insisted when he first pooh-poohed our reason for being there.

"I would love to see evidence collected from the department, ladies, not evidence from two citizens who broke into someone's house." He made it clear he wasn't happy.

"At least we brought it to you and didn't hoard it for ourselves to go see who this woman was. Besides, you already have the information Henry didn't kill him because Colonel Holz told you this morning the death occurred a few hours before the body was found, and Henry was in jail." I clamped my lips shut when I noticed his body language stiffen. "So I overheard you and Colonel talking at church."

"Overheard or eavesdropped?" He glared at me.

"Semantics." Violet grabbed the camera from my hands. "Clearly, there's a woman who came to see him. I don't know who she is, but did you check his phone records? He said something about her calling."

"Yes. We checked all phone records. He called Henry and some family members. That's it. Nothing to do with the Timberwood Project. All calls checked out." He made us well aware they were on top of everything.

"As for Henry, we are currently processing him out. I'll drop him off at the campground myself." Hank gave me a sympathetic smile. "It was good to see you at church today. Both of you."

"I'm there every Sunday." Violet's eyes popped open. "You really meant Mae." She pointed at the door. "I'm going to take my camera and myself out to wait for you in the car. Unless you're going to arrest us for breaking and entering. Then I'll wait over there." She pointed at a line of wooden chairs along the wall.

"I think I'll just forget the two of you were here."

"I'll be outside." She touched my arm and left.

"This is why I can't do this with you anymore." He gestured between us. "It's not the issue of children or who wants what—it's the fact you continue to check into things that have nothing to do with you. I understand you and Henry are friends. But, Mae, there's got to be a time when you have to stop snooping around in other's people's business and especially crimes that could potentially get you killed."

"So you're telling me that it's the part that I might get hurt that is keeping us apart, not children?" I wanted clarification to why it suddenly felt like our little break apart was being made permanent.

He stood there, stone-faced.

"I think I deserve an answer."

"This job is hard. Arresting people for robbery or petty crimes or even drugs is easy for me to disassociate from." He jabbed his chest. "My heart and people I hold in it aren't so easy for me to let go of. So when someone I care so much about that I'm willing to let go because she won't stop putting herself in danger and possibly getting killed and leaving me forever…" His voice cracked. A thin line of water clouded his pretty green eyes. "I can't deal with that."

"I can't deal with my friends who I consider family that are in danger. I need to help them."

Maybe it was the fact that I couldn't help my family when they were dying in the house fire that killed them that gave me the desire and need to help the ones I cared for when they were in trouble.

"Then we have nothing here more to discuss." He gulped back his words. "Thank you for coming in with the evidence. I will be sure we go back out to Duke's house and check out the video doorbell."

"Ahem."

I turned around and saw it was Agnes Swift who had cleared her throat to announce her arrival.

"Thank you for bringing Henry back, in case I don't get a chance to thank you then." I turned around and walked to the door, touching Agnes's shoulder on the way back.

"I'm sorry," she mouthed with a grimace of pain and watery eyes.

As much as I wanted to be happy for Henry that he was getting out, my heart had shattered into a million pieces. I considered Agnes as a granny to me as much as she was to Hank. Clearly, that relationship had ended.

Today.

"Are you okay?" Violet asked as I wiped away the tears that'd fallen between the sheriff's department and her car.

"I'm fine. I'm just so happy Henry is coming home today." I put the big fake smile on my face that I'd learned to make when I was in foster care way back when.

"Everyone loves to see a smile. Smile—it makes you feel better." I could hear Mary Elizabeth now.

Violet continued to talk about things we could do to further our investigation, but I was in no mood to discuss it.

"I know you didn't hear a word I said." Violet turned into the church parking lot and pulled up to my car. "All those *mm-hmm*s and *yeah*s were pretty much all I needed to know that something happened back there between you and Hank."

She put the car in park.

"Want to tell me about it?" she asked.

"No. I'll see you at the event later."

CHAPTER SEVENTEEN

I didn't want to tell anyone about the conversation Hank and I had at the department, much less Violet Rhinehammer. I had seen a different side of her today, but not a side that screamed best friend or even confidant.

"I can't believe it!" I squealed with delight after I pulled up to the campground and saw Betts, Mary Elizabeth, Dawn, Queenie, Dottie, Beck, Joel Grassel, Helen, and Walter Pyle all pitching in to get the campground ready for the afternoon guest arrival.

"All hands on deck!" Dottie yelled and leaned on the rake in her hand. Fifi was running around, chasing the ducks like always. I couldn't stop the huge smile on my face from growing even bigger.

I ran around the campground, doing the odds and ends that I felt were necessary, like strategically building the firewood in the fire rings so they all looked alike or even just making sure all the fire utensils were laid out the same at each campsite. It was the small details that I felt made Happy Trails Campground stand above all other campgrounds the guests could've booked to stay for the vacation.

It wasn't too long after that Hank pulled up alongside me after he'd dropped Henry off at his camper.

"I guess you've got the family you've always wanted." He slipped off his sunglasses and gestured toward all the people helping out. He gave me a genuine smile. "I'm happy for you. I think you've made the best choice."

Too bad he couldn't be included. I'd make a darn good wife and friend. I could be both, but it became clear that he didn't want both. I was going to be okay. I had to be happy for the both of us and accept Hank had come into my life when he was supposed to. Maybe it was to open my heart again for the possibility to find love or a lesson in trusting again.

I wasn't sure what it was, but there seemed to be a new season coming into my life. I wasn't sure what it was supposed to teach me, but I could feel deep in my bones there was a lesson coming to me. I'd just have to let it unfold naturally and not force it.

"Did you hear me?" Henry sidled up to me.

"I'm sorry." I shook myself out of my thoughts and focused on Henry. "What did you say?"

"I said thank you for helping me." He smiled his toothless grin and gestured for me to join the Laundry Club Ladies, taking a break on the dock. "I'm going to finish up my job while you ladies chat before you get busy with the new campers."

"Thanks, Henry."

Instead of heading straight over to the group, I went into the recreational building and got out a jug of Ty Randal's sweet iced tea along with some paper cups.

"Who could stand to wet their whistle?" I asked the group.

Everyone wanted some.

When I got to the Pyles, I asked, "How on earth did you two get roped into helping out?"

"My cousin Tucker mentioned Hank had arrested Henry. We knew Henry did all the heavy lifting around here. I called Mary Elizabeth to check on her this morning after the fire last night and since I didn't see her at church. She said she was getting herself together to come help you out." Helen's hair was more of an orange to Dottie's blood-red hair

—both of them out of a bottle and both of them put on their heads by Helen.

They were two peas in a pod, with their bedazzled tank tops on.

"I just do what I'm told." Walter snickered.

"He's a good one." Helen winked and reached over to give Walter a little pat on his hand. "I know you'll find you a good one too."

"Let's hope so because I've got to have another wedding to redo the last one." Mary Elizabeth made all of us laugh. "Henry said he'd come by tonight and take a look at the bed-and-breakfast."

"Oh good. Count me in on helping any way I can." I wanted Mary Elizabeth to know that I was there to help no matter what.

"Go on. Don't leave us in suspense. What did you find out today?" Mary Elizabeth asked as everyone tuned me in. "Henry said you came down to the station today."

I told them how I'd overheard Colonel Holz and Hank talking about the initial autopsy and how it led me to knowing for sure Henry didn't kill him. I gave them a brief rundown on Violet's wicked ability to use a bobby pin to break into a house. Then I told them how anything on the video was pretty much not going to help the case and Hank didn't seem interested in the woman Duke entertained, so our breaking and entering, though exciting, was pretty much a bust.

"Violet was right about one thing," I mentioned. "She said everyone was at the wedding, so if we figure out who wasn't at the wedding from the community, we'd possibly have the killer."

Mary Elizabeth made a startling observation. "Everyone was at the wedding. Everyone but her."

CHAPTER EIGHTEEN

When the first new guests for the week rolled into the campground with their fancy Mercedes camper van, they started the onslaught of guests for the week.

Normally, I would've welcomed them to the campground and invited them into the office while Dottie got them to sign their rental contract. They would also get a map of the campground, along with the events schedule for the week for Happy Trails and around Normal. The map also listed all the trails located around the campground. Also in their packet was the brochure the entire Daniel Boone National Park office put together with the various coupons that Rebecca had dropped off the other day.

Today, there was a line of RVs trying to get in, so Dottie had to go down the driveway for the first few guests and their paperwork while I went down the line doing the same for the next few guests. We were a well-oiled machine until we got all the reservations completed, leaving me twenty minutes to get Fifi settled and me dressed for the ribbon-cutting ceremony.

Fifi was worn out by the time she'd gobbled up her kibble.

"I guess running around all day did you some good." I sat down on the couch next to her and gave her some good rubs. "You be a good girl while I'm gone. I'll be back in a couple of hours."

I knew it wasn't going to be long. I had made a plan based on other ribbon-cutting ceremonies I'd been to and hoped Andrea Burt would be in the lineup of people standing there with the big scissors for the big photo op for Violet Rhinehammer, who was going to be there on behalf of the *Normal Gazette* and Channel 2 news. While Violet kept them busy with smiling faces and a few questions for the news, I thought it would keep them occupied just long enough for me to head inside the only building on the logging site, the trailer, and just look around.

When I finally got there, I ran my hand down the purple sundress I'd thrown on for the occasion, to get out any wrinkles it'd accumulated on the drive over. There was no way my hair was going to cooperate, with the humidity, so I put my sunglasses on top of my head and used them keep the unruly curls out of my eyes, hoping it looked somewhat fashionable.

I found Tucker at the back of the crowd while the speeches were going on. "Thanks for telling Helen and Walter about Henry."

There were speeches from not only the logging group but also a few of the environmental groups, including Environmental Group for Animal Habitats. Like most logging events, there were still protestors chanting that no matter how much data was collected, logging was bad.

No matter what side you were on, most of the time, these protestors were ignored, and per usual, the ribbon-ceremony events continued as planned.

"It's the least I could do with the information you gave me at the sheriff's department." Tucker tried to fit in with the crowd as though he weren't undercover. "Even though Henry didn't realize it was not something he was supposed to be doing, I'm still going to have to charge him with illegal logging, but it'll be a fine."

"I knew he couldn't get completely off, and I'm good with that. I'm just not good with him going to jail over a crime he didn't commit." There was a total difference, though it would be on Henry's record. I was sure he'd learned his lesson about taking odd jobs for people before checking everything out.

"I'm glad we heard the video you found, and I mean 'found' loosely, that also proved Henry didn't realize it was illegal, so I'm hoping for a fine and no penalty record for him. I'll plead his case with the judge." Tucker took a couple of steps to the right to let Rebecca join us.

"That's kind of you."

"It still doesn't get you off the bet we made." He snickered.

"Oh, a bet?" Rebecca questioned. "This sounds good."

"Mae had a theory about the case, and—" he started to tell her.

"Don't be giving out my theory," I teased and stopped him from talking. "Give me time." I still planned on moving ahead with trying to find out who'd killed Duke. As much as I didn't want to think it was possible, Mary Elizabeth had put in my head how Violet Rhinehammer hadn't been at the wedding. She'd told me she had the Henry case of illegal logging to look into.

Did she look into it and happen upon the logging site, where she and Duke could've gotten into it?

My attention jerked to the stage, where they were announcing the ribbon-cutting ceremony.

"I've got to go potty. Do you think they have a bathroom in the trailer?" I asked them.

"I don't think job trailers have bathrooms, but there's a port-a-let over there." Rebecca pointed before she turned her attention back to the ceremony while I slipped off without saying anything.

I glanced around to make sure no one noticed me walking up the three wooden steps to the trailer. I slipped inside, quietly closing the door behind me.

The lights buzzed. The police scanner had static on it and was sitting on the desk. The desk had big sheets of the layout of Daniel Boone National Park scattered over it, like on a draftsman's desk, only it was the forest instead of a building. "Timberwood Project" was stamped on each one.

There weren't any filing cabinets to look through and no desk drawers—pretty much nothing.

The door flung open, catching me off guard.

"Sorry. I was hoping there was a bathroom in here." I jumped around to find Rebecca standing in the door. "Gosh. You scared me. You were right. No bathroom."

She laughed.

"Yeah. I've had to deliver papers to these types of trailers a lot, and from experience, I knew most of them don't have bathrooms. Typically, a small desk, coffee pot, and lights before they move to the next logging site." She pointed at all the various things, and she was right. "I have to get back to the office. I threw my purse in here."

She reached down and picked up one of the few purses on the floor.

My eyes followed, in slow motion, as she slid the strap of the purse up her arm and set it on her shoulder.

"Well, I guess I better get out there for the ceremony." I tried to steady my voice as I realized that was the purse I'd seen on Duke's video. Not that I thought that made her a suspect or that she killed him, but how did she know him?

"I thought you had to go to the bathroom." She tilted her head and looked at me. "Oh my goodness, were you in here snooping?" She shook a finger at me. "I can't believe it. I'm seeing it in person. I told you I told Tucker you were so good at this." She twisted around and started all the rambling again like she always did, making me confused. "You think Andrea did it, don't you? Oh, I can see that. They are always competing against bids, and you know Andrea always beats him out. I bet she got tired of him and killed him, but how did she get the ax?"

The ax. I gulped.

"She didn't. You did." I blinked a few times as the scenario played out. "You knew somehow Duke had hired Henry, and when you came to the campground to drop off the brochures, you knew you needed something to frame Henry, so you must've gone into the storage shed and grabbed the ax."

"May-bell-ine." She tsked. Her demeanor changed, and she was deliberately picking her words and not yammering on. "Can I call you May-bell-ine?"

"I'd prefer Mae," I corrected her. "Why? Why did you do it?"

"Are you sure you want to go down this road? I'm happy to forget you were in here looking for a bathroom and to step aside so you can walk out and never question this again." She was offering me a deal, but why?

"I'll keep that thought in mind, but I really want to know why you killed Duke." It would buy me some time to think on how I could get to Hank or possibly Tucker, who was just outside.

"Duke is my cousin. He has always tried to use me to get his little deals passed by the committee. He had even given me some money as a bribe to get a few deals in front of the committee. This was all before you were appointed, but Duke never forgot that. In fact, my dear sweet cousin even used me once to smuggle some illegal hunting weapons through the office, and he was holding that against me. I was tired of being on the losing end, so when I got a sweeter offer from Andrea, I took her deal and put the Timberwood Project on your committee agenda. Lucky for me, it got passed, and I got a little kickback." An evil laugh escaped her. "Duke was so mad. He threatened to turn me in for all the bribes I took, and well, I couldn't have that. I guess when you started meddling, it had become very clear you weren't going to let Henry's case go to trial and possibly be convicted, naming Duke as his employer, so I had to do something." She thought she had it figured out.

"I like to think of myself as helping, not meddling," I corrected her. "Now that I know why you killed him, I'll take the deal you gave me about forgetting all about it." I took a step forward.

She took a step sideways to stand in front of the door.

"I'm not good at chess."

"Lucky for me"—she slipped the purse off her shoulder and pulled out a little pistol—"I kept one of those guns Duke had me smuggle." She pointed it directly at me.

"Listen, Rebecca. I didn't say Duke didn't have a reason to get killed. I don't blame you."

A shot rang out, the bullet barely missing my head.

"What are you doing?" I jerked around in panic and looked at the small hole in the trailer door. "Are you crazy? You could've killed me."

There were screams echoing outside.

"They all could hear that." I pleaded with her, "Just stop, and everything will be fine."

"I'm trying to kill you!" She knocked off another shot. I darted under the desk for cover as the police scanner buzzed with Agnes's voice.

"All deputies respond to shot fired at the logging site." Agnes didn't even give a code. Her voice was steady. I could only imagine how she would sound if she knew it was me on the other side of those shots.

"Ten seventy-six." Hearing Hank's voice come over the scanner, letting Agnes know he was on his way, did make me feel better, but Rebecca standing over me with the gun pointing down on me didn't.

"Hold it right there, Rebecca." Tucker stood at the door of the trailer. "There's no getting out of this even if you do shoot Mae. I just got word from the sheriff that you are related to Duke, and the phone records showed you talked to him a lot over the past couple of weeks. Andrea Burt just confirmed when I told her it was you in here that she did use you to get in front of the committee with the Timberwood Project proposal, so no matter what you do or decision you make, you're caught."

Rebecca's body was still. Her eyes furiously blinked at me. As she took a couple of quick breaths, her eyes closed, and she dropped the gun.

CHAPTER NINETEEN

I had nothing against trees. In fact, I wouldn't have had Happy Trails Campground if it weren't for everyone's love of trees, forests, and all nature that lies hidden beneath the branches.

And keeping my bet that I'd made with Tucker meant if I was wrong about my theory about Henry, I'd take Tucker on some of the more used trails for the rangers, but if he was right, he had to make me the Kentucky bourbon pie himself.

Now, with Rebecca behind bars and things having settled down in Normal, today was the day I was going to hold him to that promise and get that pie, but I also agreed I'd take him on a trail or two. And since it was Sunday morning, I figured it was as good a time as any for me to be gone from the campground a few hours.

A few strands of my hair were plastered to the side of my face.

"Yuck." I winced as I ripped them off, figuring I'd take the spit-pasted hair with the good night's sleep I'd gotten.

The echoes of camper screen doors screeching and slamming was a sure sign there was life going on outside. I peeled back the curtain and looked around at the campground from the bedroom window.

The sound of wheels crunching over the gravel, along with the roar of big dually trucks' engines, was another sure sound of guests packing up and heading out, either on their next adventure or back to their real life.

"I guess we better get up." I looked over at Fifi. She, too, was exhausted. "Maybe I can text Hank to see if we can get Chester for the day."

Her ears perked up at the sound of Chester's name.

"Yeah. I miss him too." I ran my hand down her back before I tossed the covers off myself and put my feet on the ground.

I wasn't going to bother getting a full shower and dressing in anything other than my cargo hiking shorts, Happy Trails Campground sweatshirt, and hiking boots. With a little water thrown on my face and some sunscreen rubbed on my cheeks, along with brushing my teeth, I was set to go on the hike.

"You ready to go potty?" I asked Fifi as she patiently stood at the door. "Come on." I opened the door so she could bolt out.

Peeling a hair tie off my wrist, I took my curly hair in one hand and made a quick knot ponytail on top of my head. The heat and humidity were going to be up there today, and curly hair made it almost impossible to be outside if it wasn't off my neck.

Before I went outside, I poured myself a cup of coffee and grabbed my backpack, which I'd already filled with the things I was going to need today.

The sun had already popped up earlier this morning over the mountain. The sky was clear blue. Snapping came from the underbrush of the forest behind my camper van, a sure sign of animals scampering around.

"Come on back! A little more." I heard one of the guests as they stood out next to a fifth-wheel hitch, gesturing the driver of a truck to come on back so they could hook up and pull out.

"You need anything?" I asked as I passed by.

"No. We wish we could stay longer." The guest waved.

"Be sure to stop by the recreation building and grab some donuts and coffee on your way out." I waved them goodbye and followed Fifi up to the front of the campground, passing more guests who were either enjoying their last few minutes of the landscape that dearly embraced them during their stay or packing things up in the storage compartments on the outsides of their campers.

Leaving day always filled me with sadness and hope. I was sad to see the guests who I'd come to live with for the past week or so go, but I held hope and gratitude that I'd met them along the way. Plus, this afternoon would bring a new crop of guests that would equally fill me with joy from learning about them and why they decided to vacation in the Daniel Boone National Forest.

Henry and Dottie were sitting at a picnic table up underneath the outside of the recreation building. Both were holding cups of coffee.

"Mornin'," Dottie greeted me. "Good to have this feller back." She snickered as she referred to Henry.

"It sure is." I patted him on the back. "Fifi missed you too."

"I reckon she did." Henry looked down at Fifi. She stood on her hind legs with her front paws on his shin. "I missed all of y'all. And this." He lifted his chin toward the mountain.

The craggy cliffs, stones, and boulders filled part of the skyline, along with all the jagged trees that made what we called home.

I sat down in an empty camping chair.

"Now that the wedding is over and there's nothing left to distract you from your feelings, what are you going to do about Hank?" Dottie glanced at me.

I eased back in the chair and, with my toes, pushed the camping chair back on its two hind legs.

I stared into the campfire. The red-and-blue flames tangoed.

"Good question." I sighed and looked over at Henry, sure he'd told her about the conversation Hank and I had when I'd gone to break Henry out of jail the second time. "I guess I have all of this and more time to be with my friends."

A truck with a green strip underneath the doors running along both sides of the white paint pulled up to the side of the recreation building. The arrowhead decal with the words "US Park Ranger" printed next to it, as well as a logo of a badge with Law Enforcement written on the side of the bed of the truck, screamed Tucker.

"What is he doin' here?" Dottie must've gotten nervous. She picked up her cigarette case and unsnapped it, then took out a smoke and lit it up.

"That's our ride." I stood up and picked Fifi up.

"Your what?" Dottie's smirked. "Well, May-bell-ine."

"It's nothing like that," I assured her. "As a committee member, Lloyd Hornbuckle had appointed me to show Tucker around a few of the trails."

We shifted our focus to a couple of trucks driving past slowly, their drivers maneuvering their campers around the lake, giving a wave to us on their way out.

"Good morning." Tucker smiled as bright as the sun shining over our heads. "Wow. This would be stunning to wake up to every day." His chin lifted in the air, and he sucked in a big, deep breath. "We didn't have these kinds of sights near Mammoth Cave." He shifted his focus to Henry. "Are you doing okay, Henry?"

"Yes, sir. I'm fine." Henry set his coffee cup on top of the picnic table. "I better get to my job. We've got a whole slew of new guests coming this week. We are going to be packed to the gills."

"Then I guess I better get the paperwork done for them." Dottie grabbed Henry's mug too. Her cigarette dangled from her mouth. Her eyes seared into Tucker throughout her entire stroll to the office.

"I'm guessing she doesn't like me." Tucker reached out and scratched Fifi on the head.

"Dottie just has to get to know you first, and right now she doesn't know you all that well." I shrugged.

"I saved you from getting killed a few weeks ago. You'd think she'd be grateful." He groaned and pointed toward his truck. "Are you ready?"

"We are." I walked over to the truck with Fifi snuggled in my arms.

"Your dog is going?" His eyes slid across the hood of his truck at me.

"One thing you need to know about me and Fifi: we are always together, and she loves to hike."

A slight grin crossed his lips, and he shrugged, getting into the truck.

"I thought we could head down to Sky Bridge. I think the ranger station gets a lot of calls for that trail." I was trying to take him places he'd need to know forward and backward without a map. "It runs along the Red River Gorge. Some of the trail is blacktopped, which a lot of older hikers or people with children like. But the seventy-five steps to get to the top of the rock-formation bridge sometimes makes the hikers need assistance."

"Sounds good." He got out his paper map.

"Why aren't you using your phone GPS?" I questioned.

"Sometimes those darn things don't get or give accurate service, so I like to pull out a real map so I can see the lay of the land." He poked the map and threw the truck into drive.

He flipped on the radio, which told me he wasn't much of a conversationalist or didn't want to talk. We were here for business anyways.

"We'd like to thank the community for coming together to help solve this crime. Logging is very important to our life here in the Daniel Boone National Forest. There's a right way and a wrong way to log. That is why we have the laws in place that we have. So if you ever see or hear anything about logging going on around your neck of the woods, you can go online or call the National Park Committee to see if they are working with an environmental group or the Kentucky Environmental Agency to see if the logging you're witnessing is an approved procedure." I found it odd to hear Deputy Al Hemmer giving the update on the radio about the case being finalized.

"You heard it here first. Remember to tune in to the five-o'clock news tonight on Channel Two, where you'll get the latest updates in and around the Daniel Boone National Park. I'm Violet Rhinehammer."

The news conference segued directly back to the music, and we didn't even talk until after Tucker had pulled his truck into the parking lot of Sky Bridge.

When we got out of the truck, Tucker walked over to the monument with the information about the trail we were about to take.

"You know, the Gorge is every ranger's dream. I mean, it was formed over three hundred million years ago," Tucker spoke with pride about his new post.

"And the Sky Bridge is actually made of sandstone." I knew I didn't have to tell him how sandstone stood the test of those millions of years as the other sediments, clays, and rocks had washed away from the river, since sandstone resisted any sort of erosion due to how hard of a rock its compound was.

"Amazing. I can't wait to see it." He used his thumbs to hike his backpack up higher on his shoulders. "Ready?"

I bent down and clipped Fifi's harness around her chest since the terrain was steep at times, and I certainly didn't want her going off any cliffs.

"Where are you going?" he asked when I walked toward a different, less-traveled trail opposite where the Sky Bridge trailhead started.

"I've got a slightly different trail that will get us there but has better views and is less traveled." I pointed. "I think you need to see Creation Falls too. We can take Rock Bridge Trail."

"Umkay." He passed by me and headed down the battered-down grassy path on the opposite side of the parking lot.

Fifi happily followed along behind him, her little legs going as fast as they could to keep up with him. Tucker used his walking stick to dart off and on the trail as though he was doing more of a workout than getting to know the trail.

The sun trickled through little peeps in the full cover of leaves of the forest, giving us enough light and shade to enjoy a nice hike down to Creation Falls, where the tree line opened up for the sun to shine on the glorious natural creation.

"This is a great trail," Tucker said as I approached.

"I love it." My words made him turn around.

He put a finger up to his mouth and showed me a little tape recorder. "The scenery is diverse. There are plenty of elevation changes. The park keeps the trail well maintained and marked. Trail number two hundred and nineteen, Swift Creek Camp, looks to be fairly accessible from the Celestial Falls as well." He clicked the button and turned to me. "Thanks, this is a great one. I like to talk into my microphone so I can capture the tone of my voice. It helps cement all of this in my head."

He never once mentioned the gorgeous three-tiered elevations of the falls as they swept over the limestone formations between the lime-green forest walls and settled into a clear pool.

Several hikers were sitting in the water along with their dogs, taking a nice break or even just washing off after camping in the forest.

Fifi and I took a walk to the edge of the falls while Tucker talked to the hikers. I made the mistake of taking Fifi off her harness. She jumped into the pool of water and darted off into the woods on the other side.

"Fifi! No!" I jumped in, regardless of getting soaked, and made my way across the water.

In the background, I heard Tucker excuse himself, and his heavy footsteps echoed behind me.

I darted in and out of the thick trees with my eyes set on the little ball of white until I got to the edge of a clearing.

"Hhhuuu," I gasped. My jaw fell open. Fifi was barking, but it sounded muffled as I took in what I was seeing.

I would know Hank's camper and truck anywhere. I'd seen the tail-lights heading out once, and now I was seeing them again. He was just rounding the corner, and I was sure he hadn't noticed us.

Fifi darted around what looked to be Hank's campsite and sniffed at what seemed to be every blade of grass.

"Did you smell Chester?" I asked and walked over to her. I dragged my foot in the indentations of the camper tires that looked like they had been there for a while.

"You're fast." Tucker emerged from the woods. He stopped next to me and shifted his gaze to see what I was looking at. "What did she smell?"

"Hank. Chester." If I tried hard enough, there was a lingering smell of Hank in the air. "Do you have that paper map on you?"

"Yeah." He pulled one strap of the backpack off his shoulders and swung the backpack around to his front. He unzipped the top and handed me the map.

"Where are we?" I asked him to show me.

"Right here." He pointed. "Soggy—" he started to say.

"Soggy Bottom," I whispered. "I guess Hank is moving out."

"You mean moving on." He took the map from me and didn't pay a bit of attention to the reaction I was having.

"Moving on?" My mouth dried. I couldn't swallow.

"Yeah. Oh." Tucker took a step back and looked at me, hoisting his backpack on his back at the same time. "By the look on your face, I'm guessing you didn't know he took the job post for the open ranger position at Mammoth Cave." He adjusted his straps to snug the pack for the hike back. "I'm sorry. My cousin told me you two had a thing, and by the way you look, she failed to tell me it was more than that."

"I'm fine. We are fine." I smiled but in the back of my head secretly sent good wishes Hank's way. "He's a great guy. He deserves to do what he loves."

No wonder Al Hemmer had done the breaking-news report we heard on the radio on our way here.

There was a realization Hank Sharp was gone—maybe gone forever —but I knew I was thankful for the time we'd passed in our lives. I truly believed there was a reason everyone came into our lives and left our lives.

For me, Hank helped me gain a love and respect for the Daniel Boone National Forest, but it was the Laundry Club Ladies who helped me gain my footing and the confidence to be the Maybelline Grant West who stood on her own two feet and didn't compromise her values. To them, I would be forever grateful.

"You ready to go back?" I focused on Tucker.

"Sure. I'm starving." He turned to lead the way. Fifi followed behind him, then I followed.

"Ty Randal serves an amazing fried-bologna sandwich that we can enjoy while you make me that pie."

Tucker turned around and smiled.

"Goodness, I've not had a fried-bologna sandwich since I was a kid. I'm game." He darted off into the woods, leaving me standing there with a smile on my face. "I'm not sure the pie I'm about to make you will be edible. I'm just warning you."

It was exciting, seeing the Daniel Boone National Park through fresh eyes.

THE END

If you enjoyed reading this book as much as I enjoyed writing it then be sure to return to the Amazon page and leave a review.

Go to Tonyakappes.com for a full reading order of my novels and while there join my newsletter. You can also find links to Facebook, Instagram and Goodreads.

Want more of Mae West and the Laundry Club Ladies?

The next book in the series, BLOSSOMS, BARBEQUE, & BLACK-MAIL is available to purchase or read in Kindle Unlimited. And read on for a sneak peek.

Chapter One of Book Twenty
Blossoms, Barbeque, & Blackmail

The lazy heat drifting up from the water told me it was time for me to paddle the kayak back to the shore. I'd drifted long enough down the stream that ran along the front of the Red Fox Trail, the trail that led straight up to Happy Trails Campground.

I was living the old saying about camping being good therapy. After all, I'd been keeping myself busy after the last few months so I didn't think about Hank Sharp's, my ex-boyfriend, moving away to take a job clear across the state of Kentucky. Now that I've settled into the fact he wasn't coming back and letting myself feel the feelings, I'd taken that old saying seriously.

The bubbles rippled up through the water made me smile at the fact there was so much life to explore in the Daniel Boone National Forest and not just as the owner of Happy Trails Campground. Letting myself take on new adventures, like laying in a kayak for hours, was something new to me. I was always on the go-go-go and making sure everyone around me was okay that I'd completely neglected myself.

I reached down next to me to grab the oar. Laughter echoed off the tall trees reminding me that even deep in the woods I wasn't alone. A couple of swipes of the water with my oar to the right and then to the left, repeating the pattern over and over as the kayak slide across the water upstream was a good workout. Only stopping for a moment to take in the waterfall and watch as the water lapped over the stone edges to settle in the pool where a family of hooded mergansers were enjoying themselves.

Yip! Fifi, my toy poodle, wanted to say hello to the duck family before she decided to join them, jumping out of the kayak and into the water.

"Fifi, get back here."

I shifted course by maneuvering my oar to paddle in her direction. Her little head bobbled up over the water's surface. She was so lazy, she knew her hot pink lifejacket would keep her above water, so she spent her energy on talking to the ducks before they decided they wanted nothing to do with her and flew off.

"I told you to stay." I reached over the side and grabbed hold of the lifejacket, pulling her wet body back into the kayak. "You just never listen." I pulled the beach towel from underneath me and wrapped her up in it to sop up the water.

She shook, spraying the extra water I'd not gotten with the towel off, sending droplets all over me.

"Pft, pft." I spit and held my hands up to my face to try and shiel any from going into my mouth.

Now paddling a little faster to get to back to Red Fox Trail, Fifi decided her little swim was enough to lay on the towel and let the sun send her off into a little nap, which she was going to need her sleep. And this little rest was much needed for myself because once I hiked back up the trail to the campground, I was going to be all sorts of busy with tonight's campground kickoff for my camping guests to this week-end's Blossom Festival.

The Tour Southern and Eastern Kentucky Association was a group who hosted tours throughout Kentucky that traditionally featured the gorgeous springtime redbuds in and around the Bluegrass state. As a tourist town, Normal, where hiking and camping was our main economic income, we capitalized on the associations tour by hosting what we called Blossom Festival.

It was a taking place this weekend with most of the festival activities being hosted in downtown Normal, mainly in the grassy median area.

The water shoes were a lifesaver and saved my feet from not only slipping but getting poked by the uneven rocks when I hopped out at the banks to pull the kayak to dry land.

"Thanks," I said to the young man who worked for Alvin Deters when he came to get the oars and kayak from me.

Alvin Deters and I had gone into business since the trail was located on my property that dumped down to the stream. Alvin was a local man who owned Deters Feed N Seed. He was once a kayak champion in his younger years which made him a perfect person to go into business with the opportunity to use the stream on the trail for an extra-curricular activity for my guests. Though Alvin was in his later years of life, he enjoyed teaching kayak lessons to families that stayed at Happy Trails Campground when he wasn't running the Feed N Seed.

"Let's go Fifi." I called her to join me on the hike back up the trail.

She barked and chased the squirrels as she darted past me, chasing them into the woods just off the edge of the path. The sunlight freckled my skin without the sweltering heat of the summer weather. Though I couldn't see Fifi, I could hear her barking.

The dry leaves crunched under my water shoes with each step closer to the campground. Before too long I'd be joining the group with the sound of laughter that fluttered on the light breeze whipping down the trail.

Red Fox Trail had gotten its name long before I'd moved into the campground. From what I understood and from what I've seen over the last few years living here, red foxes did live on that side of the campground and frequented the stream of water.

During the daylight hours they were rarely seen which was okay for me to let Fifi run amok. It was when dust fell over Happy Trails, Fifi never went outside without a leash and me attached to the other end.

"Maybelline!" Dottie Swaggert, the manager of the campground, waved her hands over her bright red short hair to grab my attention as soon as I emerged from the forest. "You ain't gonna believe what I've done."

She pointed to Helen Pyle, the owner of Cute-icles Hair Salon. I could only imagine what the two of them were up to.

"Let me guess." I tapped my temple after I'd made it over to the covered shelter on the outside of the recreational building at the front of the campground. "You two are bedazzling something?"

Helen and Dottie had gotten a bedazzling machine from a yard sale and they'd been using that sucker on anything that couldn't move away from them.

"No but that would be a very good thing to do with a dress." Helen couldn't contain her grin no matter how hard she tried. "You'd be the purtiest one out there, Dottie."

Dottie looked up into the open blue sky above like she was really noodling the idea. She crossed one arm under the other and held her cigarette out, away from her body before she slowly brought it up to her mouth and took a long drag.

"Not a bad idea." She wiggled her painted on brows.

"So what dress is needing bedazzled?" I asked.

"I've just signed up to com-pete in the Ms. Blossom Festival Pageant." Dottie blowed a steady stream of smoke out of her mouth. "We can even put my winning title on the campground brochure."

"Good idea," Helen encouraged Dottie when Dottie needed zero encouragement.

"I can see it now." Dottie uncurled her arms and spread her hands out in front of her, the cigarette leaving a trail of smoke. "Ms. Blossom Festival lives here."

My phone chirped from my back pocket and it couldn't've been at a perfect time.

"Mary Elizabeth." I held the phone in the air. "Gotta take it." I hit the green button. "Hey. Thank goodness you just saved me from probably saying something to Dottie that wouldn't've been good."

"Oh good." Mary Elizabeth, my adoptive mama, said with an upbeat tone. "I've got something to tell you." She rushed to get it out. "I've entered the Ms. Blossom Festival."

"You what?" I asked so I could make sure I heard her and not replayed Dottie's bit of news.

"Yep. I'm going to win too. With my southern hospitality and good manners, I just know I will woo the judges."

Oh dear me oh my, I sure didn't misunderstand her.

"It's going to be amazing. Not only will I get an interview with Channel 2 and a spread in the National Park Magazine as well as the Normal Gazette, I will get a five thousand dollar grand prize! Five thousand dollars!" Mary Elizabeth squealed. "That is the exact cost of the repairs from the fire."

I glanced over at Dottie. Helen Pyle had her fingertips plunged into Dottie's short red hair, pulling it up, taking a look at it, then using her fingertips to shake it out.

"I swear my ability to forgive Dottie for what she did is paying off in spades." Mary Elizabeth was the co-owner of the Milkery with was the local dairy farm which had a bed-and-breakfast. When my foster brother married my dear friend Abby, Dottie had accidentally light one of the rooms at the bed-and-breakfast on fire when she decided to smoke.

Mary Elizabeth had been in such a shock the following days after, that it took her a minute to register Dottie was smoking inside when it was strictly prohibited. Since then, Mary Elizabeth had been a little bitter about it, okay, a lot of bitter and things between them had been tense.

Mary Elizabeth had refused to hang out with my group of friends, the Laundry Club Ladies, which Dottie was a big part of and now they both were going to be contestants in the Ms. Blossom Festival?

"May-bell-ine!" Dottie hollered at me. I pulled the phone down to my neck to see what she was saying. "I'm gonna git me a new do!" She pointed to her hair as Helen grinned from ear to ear.

I gave her the okay sign with my fingers and went back to the phone call with Mary Elizabeth. There was no way I could deal with both of them doing the pageant. I never ever would've thought the two of them would have interest in the sixty years and up pageant.

"Isn't the pageant tomorrow night?" I questioned and looked to the entrance of the campground when I heard a car.

"Mmmhh, I got in just before the deadline closed today at lunch and just got word I have been entered. So tonight when I come for the party, I'm going to need your fashion eye on how I walk. You had lived in New York City and all your swanky friends there, I'm sure you've been to plenty of fashion shows that had those catwalks. Plus, all of those manner and etiquette lessons you attended when you were in high school is still the standard today."

I hated to burst her bubble, but I never attended any sort of pageant nor did I ever want to be in a pageant, but she was right about one thing from my past life in the city, I did go to a lot of fashion shows. Looking back, I was sure my ex-now-dead husband, Paul, had sent me to those fashion shows to keep me occupied from finding out about his criminal ways.

"I'll be over with my potato salad." She hung up the phone.

I wandered up to the office to greet Ethel Biddle and her bandmates of Blue Ethel and the Adolescent Farm Boys when their station wagon pulled around the corner of the building and parked next to the recreational building where they'd be setting for their music gig.

Adolescent was used very loosely.

"How's the newlyweds?" Otis Gullett, the fiddle player asked about Bobby Ray and Abby.

"You'll be able to ask them yourself tonight. They'll be here any minute." I was especially anticipating Bobby Ray coming over since I'd not seen a whole lot of him lately.

When he got married, he moved out of the bungalow in the campground and bought the very cheap model home across the street from Ava Cox, a local lawyer, where he and Abby live now.

"Rosco!" Ethel's dog jumped out of station wagon. "Fifi will be so happy to see you."

"That's a change." Ethel knew I had a little beef against Rosco when he couldn't keep to himself when she brought him to the campground during her first gig when I was babysitting Fifi. Yep. I didn't own Fifi at one time, but Rosco changed that.

Fifi was a very prestigious show dog, nationally recognized by the Kennel Club Association. She'd come from a long line of winners and her breed line was flawless until Rosco.

"If it weren't for Rosco and his male dog ways, I wouldn't've been given Fifi." It was a real catch twenty-two. At the time I was terrified to tell Tammy Jo, Fifi's original owner, but when she discarded Fifi after she was with little baby puppies, to me, I wasn't sure how to care for a dog full time much less one that was prissy and pregnant.

It turned out to be a good thing because it taught me to care for something other than myself. I'd like to think I wasn't selfish before Fifi, but now I could see I was pretty selfish and only really took care of me. I'd like to think Fifi changed me for the better.

In other words, I had Rosco to thank for that.

"Come on Rosco. Let's go find Fifi," I whistled for Rosco. He trotted down the campground road with me.

Happy Trails Campground was a full service campground that offered lots to all classes of RVs. Most of those lots were in a large circle around the lake located in the middle of the campground and just past the office and recreational building.

We also had a tent only section in the back and off to the left of the main campground just past the few bungalows we also rented.

Me, Dottie, Ty Randal, and Henry Bryant all made Happy Trails our fulltime home. Ty was the only one who didn't work for me but owned the Normal Diner and was supplying the hamburgers for tonight's grill out.

"Let me know if you need any more firewood," I told one of the guests who was stoking up their campfire. "We have plenty," I assured them.

Henry, my handyman, was priceless. He took pride in making sure all the campers had everything they needed after they checked in at the office. Since we were a full service hook up, we practically stayed full year around.

"I smell something good," I sang to another guest who had a big pot over their campfire for the big party.

Every month I hosted a campground party that was open to the locals. I loved how everyone came out to listen to the bluegrass music of Blue Ethel and the Adolescent Farm Boys while they walked around and sampled what each camper was making over their fire.

It was a great way to walk around and get to know people. I offered the main course, while everyone else cooked a side dish. People in the community, like Mary Elizabeth and her potato salad, would also bring a dish to put on the community table for the taking.

The dessert table was my favorite. And tonight's tasty sweets were compliments of Christine Watson, the owner of the Cookie Crumble Bakery.

Roscoe darted ahead of me when he saw Fifi before I did. They jumped around and took turns sniffing each other's back sides. I wondered if Fifi remembered he was her pups daddy before I shoved it in the back of my head when cackling echoed throughout the campground making me look over my shoulder.

The Laundry Club Ladies had arrived and all of them laughing at Dottie who'd obviously told them she was going to participate in the pageant and doing her best one foot in front of the other walk, hand on her hip down the pier that jutted out into the lake.

I continued to make my way around the lake and greet the guests, taking a few looks into their campfire cooking pots.

"Good evenin'! Welcome to the paarrrteee!" Blue Ethel shrieked from the microphone. "Hit it, boys!" She threw her hand up in the air signaling their very first song.

Seeing a few guest already on the plywood dance floor in front of the stage made my heart sing. I knew it was going to be a great night and this group of campers were going to be fun.

Over the past couple of years my guests had started to vary in age. I had the retired full timers to the young newlyweds as well as families. There seemed to be a good mix and I was happy to see how all the generations came together.

Blissful.

"I don't believe it," Mary Elizabeth spat as she popped off the lid to her homemade. "Did you know Dottie is going to compete?" Mary Elizabeth scoffed. "My goodness." She fiddled with the pearls around her neck. "You don't think she's gonna win, do you?" she drew back. "Honestly, she's not got a mannered bone in her body. The way she flings that cigarette around and wears hot pink sponge curlers." She tsked. "Do you?"

"I'm not getting into this." I should've just walked away. I outta kick my own self in the hinny for staying.

"Maybelline Grant West," She gasped. "Are you telling me that you aren't going to support your mama? We are family."

"We all love each other and it's high time you forgive Dottie for the fire. It was taken care of and almost everything was donated, so I'm not sure why on earth you're still holding a grudge." My mouth watered when I looked down at her homemade mustard potato salad.

"If it ain't two of my favorite gals." Bobby Ray had snuck up behind us.

"Bobby Ray!" I twirled around and threw my arms around his neck.

"Why, Maybelline, I didn't get this kind of greeting from you when I showed up right over there two years ago after I'd not seen you in ten years." He grinned like a possum.

"Stop it." I playfully smacked him on the chest before Mary Elizabeth took her stab at him.

"Give me some sugga," she pulled him to her and wrapped him up in a big mama bear hug. "You ain't going to believe what's happened." She hooked her arm in the crock of Bobby Ray's and dragged him aside away from me since she was going to try to get the sympathy from him that she wasn't getting from me.

"Help," he mouthed with a grin over his shoulder.

"Ah oh, what's that all about." Abby Fawn, now Abby Bond, asked.

"Abby!" I was so happy to see her too. "You don't want to know. Tell me, how's the house?"

The two of us strolled over to the pier where Dottie was still talking about the pageant until they noticed Abby.

"She was just telling me about the house." I sat her in the middle of the group.

"It's great. I even joined the neighborhood women's club." She pulled her hands up over her mouth to shield her laughter. "I honestly can't believe how happy we are. The house is too big for us, but Bobby Ray wants to fill it with children."

"You aren't?" I looked at her belly.

"Goodness no!" She over exaggerated.

"I can't believe you bought that house." Dottie shivered. "I wouldn't buy no house where there was a murder."

"And that way of thinking is why no one wanted to buy it and why we got it cheap." Abby didn't care. "Which brings me to some news."

"Oh gosh." I held my hand to my heart. "I can't take any more news today."

Mary Elizabeth and Dottie's news about did me in.

"Bobby Ray found his birth mother," Abby said.

My posture slumped, slightly.

BLOSSOMS, BARBEQUE, & BLACKMAIL is available to purchase or read in Kindle Unlimited. Grab it today and continue your vacation in Happy Trails Campground.

RECIPES AND CAMPER HACKS FROM MAE WEST AND THE
LAUNDRY CLUB LADIES AT THE HAPPY TRAILS CAMPGROUND
IN NORMAL KENTUCKY.

Cowboy Coffee

Oh my. We ain't in the Wild West, but we do take our coffee serious while camping. Cowboy coffee is truly a delight and pretty much the easiest type of coffee you can make over a campfire.

Here is what y'all are going to need:

- Campfire
- Kettle
- Water
- Coffee grounds
- Eggshell or Salt

Yep, you read that right. Egg or salt. If you use an egg, you might get worried about salmonella, but we are going to boil the water in the kettle first. But if you want to skip the eggshell entirely, just use salt.

Directions

1. Add water to your kettle and bring it to a boil over your campfire.
2. Once the water's boiling, remove the kettle from the campfire and let it sit for about half a minute to lower the temperature a smidgen.
3. Add 2 tablespoons of ground coffee for every 8 ounces of water. This is when you'd add the eggshell or pinch of salt.
4. Stir the grounds, salt, or eggshell into the water.
5. Let it sit for 2 minutes and stir again. This is technically the brewing process.
6. Let the coffee sit for 2 more minutes.
7. After 4 minutes of brewing, sprinkle a little cold water on the grounds because this helps the grounds go down to the bottom of the kettle.

8. Pour the coffee in your mug slowly. This will keep the grounds at the bottom of the kettle.

9. Enjoy!!!

Ho-Ho Eggs

Okay, so this one the kiddos love when going camping for a breakfast treat. Some folks might call it eggs in a basket, but in Kentucky we call them Ho-Ho Eggs.

Ingredients

- Sliced bread
- Butter
- Eggs

Directions

1. Heat your skillet over the campfire and throw a little butter in to melt.
2. Butter the amount of bread you want on each side.
3. Cut a round hole in the middle of each slice of bread. Big enough for the egg yolk to sit in. The number of bread slices is up to you and how many you want to eat.
4. Fit the pieces of bread into the heated skillet. Also put in the piece of bread you made from the hole. It's perfect for sopping up cooked egg yolk.
5. Break one egg over the hole of each slice, fitting the yolk into the hole. The egg white will spread over the rest of the piece of bread, which is fine.
6. When the downside of the bread is golden, carefully flip the bread to the other side and let it brown up, cooking the egg white. Don't forget to flip over the small rounded pieces you made from the hole. Again, great for sopping up egg yolk.
7. If you want a runny yellow egg, which I love, then just make sure the bread is good and toasted on each side. If you want the yellow cooked, you simply bust the yolk after the first flip.
8. Enjoy!

Kielbasa Hash Lunch Style

A lot of times when we are camping, we rarely sit down for a big lunch because we are generally busy hiking or doing some sort of activity. When we do cook for lunch, we love to be able to make ONE skillet dishes, and this is one of those.

Ingredients

- 1 package of turkey kielbasa (or really any meat, but I like turkey)
- 1 of each: green, red, yellow, orange pepper
- 1 onion, diced
- 2 large russet potatoes
- Olive oil
- Skillet – I use cast iron over the campfire

Directions

1. Over a hot campfire, add olive oil to the skillet.
2. Add your potatoes that you've sliced up to get them brown, which is about 10 minutes.
3. Remove the potatoes when cooked brown and set aside.
4. Add sliced-up kielbasa to the skillet and add more oil if you need to. Brown the slices.
5. Remove the kielbasa after cooked and set aside.
6. In the same skillet, add the peppers and onions.
7. Once the peppers and onions are softened, add in the potatoes and kielbasa. Mix together and heat up.
8. Enjoy!

Camping Hack #1

Have y'all seen the Press-N-Seal from Glad? Well...we learned a GREAT hack from a fellow camper when we went a couple of weeks ago.

When sitting outside or even just around the campfire, bugs are out and about. It's okay. We like bugs, but we don't like them in our drinks.

Or we've been sitting at the picnic table or around the campfire and somehow the cup gets knocked over. Yep, it happens.

Here's the hack:

*buy some Glad Press-N-Seal

*Cut square pieces larger than the mouths of your cups, and you can do this before you go camping so they are ready to use.

* After you pour your drink, put the piece of Press-N-Seal over the mouth of the cup and apply pressure to the perimeter of the cup.

*It's all sealed!

*Poke a hole with a straw and start drinking! This is great for kiddos too!

Camping Hack #2

Camping can bring a lot of rust. I know that we use our camper all year around, and I even write in my camper (as you should know). Since we use it a lot, we don't get rust on our pans.

Some of our camping friends will camp during the warmer months and store their campers in the winter months which means NO cooking. Some of them also leave their cookware in the campers, which is fine, but guess what happens over time…RUST!

Now, who on earth wants to scrub all that rust when it's time to hit the road? NOT ME! I want to jump in and go!

Do you know those pesky silica packs you get in shoes and other things you order? The ones you're worried your dog or cat might eat and you immediately throw away?

Don't!

Guess what you can do with those?

Mmmhmmmm. You're right! Throw them in your cookware when not using them. It keeps the rust away. Honest!

Camping Hack #3

A little secret about me, I am scared of the dark! I know! I go camping and I'm still scared of the dark. I write mysteries and I'm still scared of the dark!

This is a great hack for a little light when camping and it's genius!

We bring along gallon jugs of water to use. We make coffee in the pot with it, cook with it, fill up Rowena's water bowl with it, what I'm saying is that we use a lot of water.

If you don't have a headlamp for camping, you need one! Not only for hiking and to light up a trail or cave, but to have for this reason. Grab your water jug and put your headlamp around it, or you can even use a water bottle. This actually works as a great light!

It's pretty cool and I hope you try it. It's also very romantic.

.

Wildlife, Weapons, & Warrants
Book Club Questions

Question 1:

Mae, along with the help of her mom, Mary Elizabeth, are hosting a bachelorette party for Abby Fawn. Abby and Bobby Ray are getting married the next day and Mary Elizabeth is in her element, creating an enchanting, fairytale event. At the end of Mae's heartfelt toast, she notices Hank pull up to Henry's camper. She doesn't think anything about it until she sees Henry in the BACK of Hank's Sheriff's car!

What were your first thoughts when this happened?

Question 2:

At the first opportunity, Mae rushes over to the jail to find out what's going on. She finds out that Henry has been arrested on illegal logging charges in the Daniel Boone National Forrest. The video clearly shows Henry cutting down the tree, not marked for logging. Henry explains he was hired by a man named Duke Weaver. They were supposed to meet at the diner to get paid, but Duke never showed. Mae's knows she needs to find an alibi to put Henry in the clear.

Did you think Henry had been framed or was it all a misunderstanding?

Question 3:

The Wedding, held at The Milkery, went off without a hitch. As soon as she could disappear, she took off on her fact-finding mission to clear Henry. By the time she returned to her camper the Laundry Club Ladies come rushing over. They have been looking all over for Mae, "grab your notebook! There's been a murder!"

What? Who could the victim be? Wasn't everyone at the wedding?

Question 4:

What was Dottie thinking? On the way to the crime scene, the ladies tell Mae about the fire at The Milkery! Dottie was smoking and tapped an ash out the window, only it flew back onto the carpet which burst into flames, taking the curtains, and wallpaper with it. Thankfully, Hank saw the situation, called on couple firefighters to put out the fire. Mary Elizabeth was understandably in shock!

How did you feel when you found out The Milkery caught fire? Were you concerned for Mary Elizabeth? Thoughts om Dottie?

Question 5:

At the crime scene, Mae and the ladies split up to get the 411 on the victim and any other info they can listen in on. While waiting for details, Violet Rhinehammer comes up behind her trying to get info for her news station and Gazette. Not only is hunky Hank investigating the scene but a new, quite handsome ranger! Tucker Pyle steps forth to make a statement about the crime, although not giving much information. Suddenly Violet is speaking up on Mae's behalf, informing the ranger who Mae is!

Ahh – a new ranger is in town, and Mae and Hank no longer a couple, what did you think of that?

Question 6:

Wow, Violet of all people, looks like Mae has a new ally wanting to pair up to investigate. In the past, Mae and Violet would clash and aren't exactly best friends. Are they even friends?

I would never have thought these two would work together to solve a murder! Thoughts on their teaming up?

Question 7:

Hank calls Mae back to the crime scene where she learns the victim is Duke Weaver, the man Henry said hired him. The murder weapon, an ax to the head! Not any ax, but one stamped with the Happy Trails Campground logo, from Henry's tool shed. Now, Henrys, alibi was dead, his ax at the crime scene, things were not looking good at this point!

Was it an accident? Who in Normal would want to frame this sweet old man?

Question 8:

Tucker tells Mae he listens to the folk in and around Normal, and their opinions on Mae. He is willing to listen to her ideas, without telling her to "stay out of the investigation!" This is new for Mae, although Hank started accepting that Mae could information since people would open up to her, it was still a major problem with their relationship.

With Tucker willing to listen, I felt like it was a validation of Mae's attention to details. Thoughts on what you were seeing with Tucker playing a new roll in Normal?

Question 9:

My favorite parts of the book are always the "Dottie-isms," and this one was no exception!

Did you have one this time?

When Dottie is talking to Betts – "You sweep your own back porch before sweeping someone else's."

Question 10:

Without telling us who it is, did you figure this one out, or was it a complete surprise? Pretty much a surprise to me. I thought I knew, then confirmed at the end.

Yes or No

A NOTE FROM TONYA

Thank y'all so much for this amazing journey we've been on with all the fun cozy mystery adventures! We've had so much fun and I can't wait to bring you a lot more of them. When I set out to write about them, I pulled from my experiences from camping, having a camper, and fond memories of camping.

Readers ask me if there's a real place like those in my books. Sadly, no. It's a combination of places I've stayed and would own if I could.
 XOXO ~ Tonya

For a full reading order of Tonya Kappes's Novels, visit
Tonyakappes.com

BOOKS BY TONYA
SOUTHERN HOSPITALITY WITH A SMIDGEN OF HOMICIDE

Camper & Criminals Cozy Mystery Series

All is good in the camper-hood until a dead body shows up in the woods.

BEACHES, BUNGALOWS, AND BURGLARIES
DESERTS, DRIVING, & DERELICTS
FORESTS, FISHING, & FORGERY
CHRISTMAS, CRIMINALS, AND CAMPERS
MOTORHOMES, MAPS, & MURDER
CANYONS, CARAVANS, & CADAVERS
HITCHES, HIDEOUTS, & HOMICIDES
ASSAILANTS, ASPHALT & ALIBIS
VALLEYS, VEHICLES & VICTIMS
SUNSETS, SABBATICAL AND SCANDAL
TENTS, TRAILS AND TURMOIL
KICKBACKS, KAYAKS, AND KIDNAPPING
GEAR, GRILLS & GUNS
EGGNOG, EXTORTION, AND EVERGREEN
ROPES, RIDDLES, & ROBBERIES
PADDLERS, PROMISES & POISON
INSECTS, IVY, & INVESTIGATIONS
OUTDOORS, OARS, & OATH
WILDLIFE, WARRANTS, & WEAPONS
BLOSSOMS, BBQ, & BLACKMAIL
LANTERNS, LAKES, & LARCENY
JACKETS, JACK-O-LANTERN, & JUSTICE
SANTA, SUNRISES, & SUSPICIONS
VISTAS, VICES, & VALENTINES
ADVENTURE, ABDUCTION, & ARREST
RANGERS, RVS, & REVENGE

CAMPFIRES, COURAGE & CONVICTS
TRAPPING, TURKEY & THANKSGIVING
GIFTS, GLAMPING & GLOCKS
ZONING, ZEALOTS, & ZIPLINES
HAMMOCKS, HANDGUNS, & HEARSAY
QUESTIONS, QUARRELS, & QUANDARY
WITNESS, WOODS, & WEDDING
ELVES, EVERGREENS, & EVIDENCE
MOONLIGHT, MARSHMALLOWS, & MANSLAUGHTER
BONFIRE, BACKPACKS, & BRAWLS

Killer Coffee Cozy Mystery Series

Welcome to the Bean Hive Coffee Shop where the gossip is just as hot as the coffee.

SCENE OF THE GRIND
MOCHA AND MURDER
FRESHLY GROUND MURDER
COLD BLOODED BREW
DECAFFEINATED SCANDAL
A KILLER LATTE
HOLIDAY ROAST MORTEM
DEAD TO THE LAST DROP
A CHARMING BLEND NOVELLA (CROSSOVER WITH MAGICAL CURES MYSTERY)
FROTHY FOUL PLAY
SPOONFUL OF MURDER
BARISTA BUMP-OFF
CAPPUCCINO CRIMINAL
MACCHIATO MURDER

Holiday Cozy Mystery Series

CELEBRATE GOOD CRIMES!

FOUR LEAF FELONY
MOTHER'S DAY MURDER
A HALLOWEEN HOMICIDE
NEW YEAR NUISANCE
CHOCOLATE BUNNY BETRAYAL
FOURTH OF JULY FORGERY
SANTA CLAUSE SURPRISE
APRIL FOOL'S ALIBI

Kenni Lowry Mystery Series

Mysteries so delicious it'll make your mouth water and leave you hankerin' for more.

FIXIN' TO DIE
SOUTHERN FRIED
AX TO GRIND
SIX FEET UNDER
DEAD AS A DOORNAIL
TANGLED UP IN TINSEL
DIGGIN' UP DIRT
BLOWIN' UP A MURDER
HEAVENS TO BRIBERY

Magical Cures Mystery Series

Welcome to Whispering Falls where magic and mystery collide.

A CHARMING CRIME
A CHARMING CURE
A CHARMING POTION (novella)
A CHARMING WISH

BOOKS BY TONYA

A CHARMING SPELL
A CHARMING MAGIC
A CHARMING SECRET
A CHARMING CHRISTMAS (novella)
A CHARMING FATALITY
A CHARMING DEATH (novella)
A CHARMING GHOST
A CHARMING HEX
A CHARMING VOODOO
A CHARMING CORPSE
A CHARMING MISFORTUNE
A CHARMING BLEND (CROSSOVER WITH A KILLER COFFEE COZY)
A CHARMING DECEPTION

Mail Carrier Cozy Mystery Series

Welcome to Sugar Creek Gap where more than the mail is being delivered.

STAMPED OUT
ADDRESS FOR MURDER
ALL SHE WROTE
RETURN TO SENDER
FIRST CLASS KILLER
POST MORTEM
DEADLY DELIVERY
RED LETTER SLAY

About Tonya

Tonya has written over 100 novels, all of which have graced numerous bestseller lists, including the USA Today. *Best known for stories charged with emotion and humor and filled with flawed characters, her novels have garnered reader praise and glowing critical reviews. She lives with her husband and a very spoiled rescue cat named Ro. Tonya grew up in the small southern Kentucky town of Nicholasville. Now that her four boys are grown men, Tonya writes full-time in her camper she calls her SHAMPER (she-camper).*

Learn more about her be sure to check out her website tonyakappes.com. Find her on Facebook, Twitter, BookBub, and Instagram

Sign up to receive her newsletter, where you'll get free books, exclusive bonus content, and news of her releases and sales.

If you liked this book, please take a few minutes to leave a review now! Authors (Tonya included) really appreciate this, and it helps draw more readers to books they might like. Thanks!

Made in United States
Troutdale, OR
12/19/2023

16126620R00096